The Silent Architect

A Journey of Vision, Resilience, and Legacy

Siddharth Jain

merchantability, fitness for a particular purpose. The Publisher and Editor shall not be liable whatsoever for any errors, omissions, whether such errors or omissions result from negligence, accident, or any other cause or claims for loss or damages of any kind, including without limitation, indirect or consequential loss or damage arising out of use, inability to use, or about the reliability, accuracy or sufficiency of the information contained in this book.

Made with 🤍 on the Notion Press Platform

www.notionpress.com

Table of Contents

Prologue

The Roots of Ambition

In Mumbai, a modest apartment, the rhythmic patter of the monsoon rain lashed against the windows, providing a soothing background to Avantika Agarwal's late-night ritual. Her workstation, which was littered with open textbooks, notepads, and a battered laptop, was illuminated by a small desk lamp. Avantika was a graduate trainee at National Progress Bank, one of the most prestigious and ancient financial institutions in India, when she was 25 years old. She was still years away from her ascent to the position of CEO, a future she could scarcely comprehend at the time. However, the seeds of her ambition were forming in those tranquil, rain-soaked evenings.

The Spark of Curiosity

Avantika had consistently demonstrated an inquisitive nature. Her early life was significantly influenced by her father's narratives of resourcefulness and resilience, as she was born and reared in a small town in Uttar Pradesh. He maintained the family's financial stability by operating a modest store that specialized in books and stationery. Her mother, a former schoolteacher, frequently supplemented the family's income by tutoring children in the community. The Agarwal household was modest, but it was brimming with a passion for education.

Avantika's exceptional aptitude for mathematics and acute intellect distinguished her from a young age. Her father frequently made light-hearted remarks, such as, "Avantika, if I had possessed your intelligence, I would have transformed this establishment into a vast empire." Although intended as a joke, his words ignited a desire within her to construct something that would endure and be significant.

Her journey to Mumbai commenced with a scholarship to a distinguished business school. She was captivated by the potential of finance to effect change, which led her to discover her passion for the field. Although her classmates perceived banking as a lucrative profession, Avantika viewed it as a means of empowerment—a means of bridging gaps, creating opportunities, and transforming lives.

First Step

When Avantika joined National Progress Bank as a trainee, she was allocated to a bustling suburban branch. Her initial responsibilities were routine: authenticating loan documents, processing customer applications, and attending an interminable number of compliance training sessions. Nevertheless, she approached each task with the utmost diligence, resolute in her pursuit of a comprehensive understanding of the complex machinery of the financial industry.

These were the years in which she first encountered the human narratives that underlie the numerical data. She encountered customers whose lives were intricately linked to the bank, including a young entrepreneur who was in search of capital for a startup, a retired teacher who was managing her savings, and a farmer who was traversing the intricacies of agricultural loans. Each interaction reinforced her conviction that banking was more than just a means of transaction; it was a source of sustenance.

A Moment of Clarity

The pivotal moment occurred during a branch meeting that was conducted by the regional manager, Mr. Ravi

Deshpande. Deshpande was a seasoned banker who was known for his fair yet firm leadership. On that day, he delivered a case study regarding a loan initiative that had failed, resulting in the branch's inability to recoup its losses.

"Does anyone have any recommendations?" Deshpande inquired, his demeanour being somewhat antagonistic. With the exception of Avantika, who tentatively raised her hand, the room fell mute.

"Sir, I believe the problem is in the manner in which we evaluate risk," she stated, her voice remaining composed in spite of her anxiety. She subsequently presented a more comprehensive approach to loan application evaluation that incorporates financial literacy and community engagement.

Deshpande listened attentively before smiling. "Avantika, you have provided me with a plethora of ideas to contemplate." We should determine whether it is feasible to transform this concept into a pilot project.

The branch's performance was not only improved by the pilot's success, but it also captivated the attention of senior executives. It was the initial indication of Avantika's potential as a visionary leader.

Ascending the Ladder

The subsequent decade witnessed Avantika's career ascent. Her ability to navigate challenges, empathetic leadership, and acute analytical skills resulted in her rapid promotions. She transitioned from branch operations to corporate strategy and subsequently directed the bank's retail division. Each position provided new insights and lessons regarding the institution's assets and weaknesses.

Prior to her appointment to the executive team, the bank was at a critical juncture. Inefficiencies, internal discord, and an inability to adapt to the digital age were obscuring its legacy as a trusted institution. Customers were favouring fintech disruptors that provided convenience and speed, as competitors were expanding their market share.

Avantika perceived these obstacles as opportunities rather than threats. She frequently advised her colleagues that "change is inevitable." "The question is, will we be the ones to lead or follow?"

The Call to Lead

The board's decision to appoint Avantika as CEO arrived during a turbulent time. The bank's reputation had been severely damaged by a whistleblower scandal, and morale was at an all-time low. There were numerous inquiries regarding her readiness to assume leadership of an organization of this magnitude.

A town hall meeting with employees was held to commemorate Avantika's inaugural day as CEO. She addressed a sceptical audience with sincerity.

"I am aware that we have encountered obstacles," she stated. "But setbacks are not failures. These opportunities are opportunities to learn, to develop, and to reconstruct. In addition to reviving this institution, we will also redefine the concept of a bank in the 21st century.

A flame was sparked by her words. She gradually reestablished trust by aligning the bank's objectives with the principles that had previously established it as a pillar of the community.

Planting the Seeds

Avantika's tenure as CEO commenced with a thorough evaluation of the bank's operations. She implemented a three-phase transformation strategy that prioritized cultural renewal, customer engagement, and digital innovation.

1. **Digital Innovation:** Utilizing AI and blockchain technology to optimize processes, improve security, and provide customized services.

2. **Customer Engagement:** Implementing initiatives such as hybrid service models and financial literacy programs to accommodate a wide range of customer requirements.

3. **Cultural Renewal:** Fostering accountability, transparency, and inclusivity within the organization.

Her objective was straightforward: to establish a bank that was both future-ready and enduring by combining the best of tradition and innovation.

A Legacy in the Making

Avantika's stewardship over the years has transformed National Progress Bank into a symbol of progress and resilience. Her journey was not without obstacles—internal resistance, economic disruptions, and cybersecurity threats all put her resolve to the test. Nevertheless, each obstacle served to bolster her conviction in the efficacy of purpose-driven leadership and collaboration.

While preparing to commemorate the bank's centennial with employees, customers, and partners, Avantika contemplates the lessons she has acquired. She has come to the realization that leadership is not about individual victories, but rather about collective accomplishments. It pertains to the establishment of opportunities for others to prosper and the establishment of a legacy that will endure.

The prologue concludes with Avantika standing by her office window, observing the rain descend over Mumbai. The city, like the bank, is a testament to resilience and reinvention. Her thoughts shift to the future as she contemplates the horizon, confident that the best is yet to come.

Chapter 1:

The Storm Within

The sun cast a golden hue on the iconic façade of "National Progress Bank," a venerable institution nestled in the bustling heart of Mumbai. Its marble pillars stood tall, exuding a legacy of trust and stability. Inside, however, the atmosphere was anything but tranquil. The corridors echoed with hurried footsteps and whispered conversations—the kind that hinted at secrets too dangerous to speak aloud.

Avantika Agarwal, a young and ambitious Assistant General Manager, sat in her corner office overlooking Marine Drive. Her path to this position had been anything but smooth. She was a product of relentless hard work, a meritocratic outlier in a system often swayed by politics and nepotism. Avantika had recently spearheaded a digital transformation initiative, earning accolades from customers and junior staff alike. But with success came enemies.

Across the hall, Ramesh Bhardwaj, the General Manager of Operations, brooded over his coffee. A veteran of the bank, Ramesh believed he was the rightful heir to the Executive Director's chair. Avantika's meteoric rise had unsettled him, and he wasn't alone. The old guard—a coterie of senior officials—felt threatened by her unconventional methods and growing influence.

"We need to clip her wings," Ramesh confided to his confidant, Neeta Sharma, the Chief of Human Resources. Neeta nodded, her eyes narrowing. She had her reasons to resent Avantika, who had exposed unethical hiring practices in a report six months earlier.

The seeds of conflict had been sown.

Chapter 2:

Whispers and Alliances

The air inside the main conference hall of National Progress Bank felt heavier than usual. A soft hum of conversation buzzed among the executives as they settled into their seats, clutching the agenda for the upcoming annual review meeting. For most, this was a routine affair; for Avantika Agarwal, it was a battlefield in disguise.

Avantika leaned back in her chair at a small café tucked away in a corner of Colaba, carefully thumbing through her presentation notes. Across from her sat Arjun Kapoor, the bank's sharp-witted Chief Technology Officer. Together, they were the architects of a bold vision—an AI-driven credit assessment system. This was no mere technology upgrade; it was a seismic shift in how the bank approached lending.

"We're taking a risk," Arjun admitted, his fingers tracing the rim of his coffee cup. "This will either make or break our credibility with the board."

"That's why we need to back every point with hard data," Avantika replied. Her voice carried an edge of determination that masked the flicker of anxiety within. "If we're going to survive the onslaught from Ramesh's camp, we'll need to show them this isn't just a gamble. It's the future."

The conversation shifted to tactics. Arjun emphasized the importance of framing the proposal in a way that pre-empted criticism, while Avantika mapped out responses to potential objections. Their collaboration was seamless, a product of mutual respect and shared ambition.

Meanwhile, in the grand office of Ramesh Bhardwaj, a different kind of meeting was underway. Ramesh had summoned Neeta Sharma and three other senior managers who had long been loyal to the old guard.

"The annual review is our chance to dismantle her little tech empire," Ramesh said, his voice cold and measured. He gestured toward a stack of documents on his desk. "These are cost analyses that highlight the financial risks of her proposal. I want each of you to memorize these figures. During the meeting, we'll bury her under questions she can't answer."

Neeta nodded, her lips curving into a thin smile. "And if she falters even once, it'll reinforce the narrative that she's out of her depth."

The group spent hours rehearsing their strategy, fuelled by a shared animosity toward Avantika's progressive ideas. For them, preserving the status quo wasn't just a matter of principle; it was a matter of survival.

As the day of the review drew nearer, tensions within the bank escalated. The atmosphere in the corridors grew thick with speculation, and whispers of alliances being forged and broken reached Avantika's ears. Yet, she kept her focus on the task at hand.

The night before the meeting, Avantika stayed late in her office, going over her presentation one last time. She glanced at the clock; it was nearing midnight. Her phone buzzed, and she saw a message from Arjun: "All set for tomorrow. We've got this."

She allowed herself a small smile. Despite the looming challenge, she knew she wasn't fighting this battle alone.

Chapter 3:

The Meeting

The boardroom on the 15th floor of National Progress Bank's headquarters was a blend of old-world elegance and modern functionality. A long mahogany table dominated the room, its surface gleaming under the sunlight streaming through floor-to-ceiling windows. Velvet drapes lined the walls, and subtle ambient lighting highlighted the intricate woodwork. Despite its luxury, the air was thick with unspoken tension.

Avantika entered the room with her laptop and a stack of neatly organized documents. Her attire, a crisp navy-blue suit, projected confidence, though inside, her nerves churned. The faint scent of freshly polished wood and leather mingled with the sharp aroma of coffee, served in pristine white porcelain cups. Arjun had arrived earlier, setting up the projector and ensuring every technical detail was perfect. Across the room, Ramesh and Neeta exchanged knowing glances, their demeanour calm, almost smug.

As the board members began to arrive, a quiet murmur filled the room. Mr. Rajan Patel, the Chairman, entered last, his imposing presence silencing the chatter. A man in his sixties with piercing eyes and a reputation for fairness, Mr. Patel was known for his ability to sway decisions with a single comment. He adjusted his glasses and settled into his chair at the head of the table, the leather creaking softly under his weight.

The meeting began with routine agenda items. Department heads presented quarterly reports, highlighting numbers and achievements. Each presentation was met with polite applause, though the undercurrent of anticipation was palpable. The room seemed to hold its breath as Avantika's turn approached.

When it was finally her time, Avantika took a deep breath, stood up, and approached the screen. The projector whirred to life, casting a bright glow that contrasted with the soft tones of the room.

"Ladies and gentlemen," she began, her voice steady despite the adrenaline coursing through her veins. "The banking industry is at a crossroads. Traditional methods are no longer sufficient to meet the demands of our rapidly evolving customer base. Today, I present to you a vision for the future of lending—a future rooted in AI-driven credit assessment."

Her presentation was a masterclass in clarity and precision. Slide after slide detailed the benefits of the proposed system: reduced default rates, faster processing times, and increased customer satisfaction. She cited examples of similar implementations in global banks, weaving in anecdotes that humanized the data. The board members leaned forward, their expressions a mix of intrigue and scepticism.

Ramesh, however, sat back in his chair, arms crossed. His smirk betrayed his intentions. He waited until Avantika had finished before clearing his throat.

"An impressive presentation, Avantika," he began, his tone laced with condescension. "However, I have concerns about the cost implications. Have you factored in the training expenses for our staff and the potential resistance from our traditional customer base?"

Avantika anticipated this. "Absolutely, Mr. Bhardwaj. Slide 14 addresses these concerns. Training costs have been accounted for in the initial budget, and our customer surveys indicate a strong preference for faster, more accessible lending processes."

Ramesh frowned but pressed on. "And what about cybersecurity risks? AI systems are known to be vulnerable to breaches. A single incident could tarnish the bank's reputation."

Arjun interjected, his tone firm. "We've partnered with leading cybersecurity firms to ensure the system's robustness. Additionally, the pilot phase includes rigorous stress testing to address such scenarios."

The exchange continued, with Ramesh and his allies raising objections that Avantika and Arjun countered with facts and logic. Mr. Patel observed quietly, his sharp gaze flicking between the speakers.

The tension in the room was almost tangible. The occasional rustle of papers and the soft hum of the projector were the only sounds as the duel of wits played out. Avantika felt the weight of every glance, every whispered comment exchanged among the board members.

Finally, Mr. Patel raised his hand, signalling for silence. "I've heard enough," he said, his voice cutting through the tension. "Avantika, your proposal is ambitious and well-researched. However, the concerns raised are valid. I propose we approve the pilot phase with close oversight. If successful, we can consider scaling up."

A murmur of agreement rippled through the room. Avantika felt a mix of relief and frustration. While her project had cleared its first hurdle, the pilot phase under Ramesh's supervision was a potential minefield.

As the meeting adjourned, Avantika caught Ramesh's smirk. "The game is on," his expression seemed to say. But Avantika was ready. The battle for the bank's future had only just begun.

This chapter now immerses the reader in the boardroom's charged atmosphere, enhancing the tension and setting the stage for the unfolding corporate battle.

Chapter 4:

The Aftermath

The morning following the board meeting, the corridors of National Progress Bank's headquarters were unusually silent. The thick glass walls of the offices reflected the pale sunlight streaming through, creating an illusion of calm that contradicted the tempest brewing within. Avantika sat in her office, the door closed, her mind replaying the events of the previous day.

A victory and a trap, the prototype phase's approval was. She was aware that the road ahead would be perilous, given the substantial weight of Ramesh's supervision. Her thoughts were consumed by strategies to mitigate the inevitable challenges, and she had barely slept the night before. She was jolted back into the present moment by the knock on her door.

"Come in," she said, her voice steady but fatigued.

Arjun entered the room with a file in his hand and a concerned expression. "You've seen the email from Ramesh's office?" he inquired, dropping the file onto her desk.

Avantika lifted the document and nodded. "An oversight committee for the pilot phase.

Ramesh is typical. The identities of the members were scanned by her. Most were loyal to Ramesh, handpicked to scrutinize every step of her endeavour.

Arjun occupied the seat opposite her. "He is not even concealing his intentions." They will attempt to worsen this situation to the greatest extent feasible.

"We anticipated this," Avantika stated, setting the file down. "However, we must remain two steps ahead." Let's commence with a team meeting this afternoon. We will allocate responsibilities and establish more stringent deadlines. It is imperative that each move be meticulously documented and transparent.

The oversight committee meeting later that week was the first measure of Avantika's resilience. The conference room, which was smaller than the boardroom, was equally intimidating due to its circular table and the unrelenting fluorescent lighting. Ramesh presided over the meeting, projecting a smug demeanour as he spelled out the terms.

He began by stating, "We will require weekly progress reports on the pilot." His voice was resonant with authority. "Prior authorization from this committee is necessary for any deviation from the approved plan."

Avantika kept her expression neutral. "Understood, Mr. Bhardwaj. We'll assure full transparency."

Ramesh's lips twitched into a grimace. "Good. This is not about personal ambitions; it is about the bank's reputation.

Avantika permitted the jab to pass, despite its thinly disguised nature. She responded with a level voice, "Certainly."

The meeting continued, with committee members raising pointed concerns about timelines, costs, and potential risks. The undercurrent of hostility was unmistakable, but Avantika's calm and detailed responses managed to keep them at bay. Ramesh was observed whispering to Neeta as the meeting concluded.

As they departed, the hallway echoed with their merriment, serving as a reminder of the obstacle that lay ahead.

In the tiny brainstorming room adjacent to her office, Avantika assembled her core team that evening. Arjun, Priya, the analytics lead, and Manish, the project manager, constituted the team. They sat around a whiteboard covered in flowcharts and post it notes, the air dense with tension and determination.

Avantika asserted with a firm demeanour, "It is not solely about pilot management." "It's about proving our capability to lead this bank into the future. Ramesh and his team will endeavour to undermine us at every turn. It is imperative that we anticipate their actions and maintain a competitive edge.

Manish acknowledged. "The project plan has already been optimized." But we'll need additional resources to satisfy the aggressive timelines."

"I'll handle that," Avantika assured him. "Priya, your team will be required to verify each data point prior to submission." No room for errors."

Priya held her notebook in one hand and leaned forward. "Understood. Additionally, I will conduct scenario analyses to anticipate potential obstacles.

"Good," Avantika said. "Also, Arjun, your team will guarantee that the technology infrastructure is flawless." "Any malfunction will serve as ammunition for them."

"Consider it done," Arjun replied.

The meeting lasted late into the night, with the team poring over details, brainstorming contingencies, and rallying around their shared objective. The room was filled with a newfound sense of purpose by the time they disbanded.

The pilot phase commenced the following week in three branches located throughout Mumbai. The AI-driven credit assessment system was subjected to a comprehensive evaluation by selecting each branch based on its distinct transaction volume and customer base. Avantika personally visited each branch to resolve the managers' concerns and provide them with a briefing.

"This isn't just a trial," she told the staff at the first branch. "It's a glimpse into the future of banking. Your feedback and cooperation will shape how we serve our customers in the years to come.".

The initially apprehensive staff were reassured by Avantika's confidence and clarity, and by the end of the day, she had won them over and secured their support for the pilot.

In the interim, the oversight committee's level of scrutiny was heightened. Ramesh demanded exhaustive weekly reports, dissecting every detail with the intent to discover flaws. Requests for additional resources were delayed in the appearance of "necessary approvals," and minor issues were exaggerated.

Avantika conscientiously documented each interaction, thereby establishing a record of the committee's activities. When a delay in resource allocation threatened to derail the timeline, she escalated the matter to Mr. Patel.

She clarified during a one-on-one meeting, "Mr. Patel, the pilot's safety is at risk due to this delay."

"We have fulfilled all of the committee's requirements; however, the absence of timely assistance is impeding our progress."

Mr. Patel's expression was contemplative as he listened attentively. "Avantika, "I'll look into it, this project is too vital to be undermined by internal politics."

In the third week of the pilot, the breakthrough occurred. The AI system flagged a potential high-risk loan application that traditional methods had cleared. The case was escalated to the branch manager, who verified the system's assessment and discovered discrepancies in the applicant's documents. The incident validated the system's efficacy and provided a tangible example of its value.

Avantika presented the findings at the next oversight committee meeting. She concluded, "This is precisely the reason we require this system." "It not only enhances efficiency but also mitigates risks that traditional methods overlook."

The committee members, including Ramesh, were forced to acknowledge the success. Despite the persistence of their inquiries, the atmosphere of the meetings began to change.

Avantika's team experienced an increase in self-assurance as the pilot phase progressed. The initial hurdles gave way to a steady rhythm, with the branches reporting improved processing times and positive customer feedback. Even Ramesh's committee members encountered difficulty in identifying deficiencies.

The pilot phase had surpassed expectations by the conclusion of the sixth week. Avantika prepared a comprehensive report for the board, detailing the outcomes, challenges, and recommendations for scaling up the system.

She permitted herself a moment of gratification as she concluded the presentation. Although the conflict was not yet concluded, she was entitled to this triumph.

The chapter concludes with Avantika standing on her office balcony, gazing out at the Mumbai skyline. The city's lights twinkled like a constellation, serving as a reminder of the boundless opportunities that lay ahead. She was prepared to advance one step at a time, despite the numerous obstacles and the length of the journey.

Chapter 5:

Shadows and Revelations

The corridors of the National Progress Bank's headquarters were full of varied reactions as the pilot phase of the AI-driven credit assessment system entered its seventh week. Although the initial reports from the branches suggested favourable results, there were rumours of dissatisfaction and suspicious errors that began to circulate. Avantika had acquired the ability to identify these murmurs as meticulously orchestrated endeavours to undermine her project.

A compact space, the analytics room was dominated by screens that displayed real-time data from the pilot branches, where Avantika stood. The cool glow of the monitors illuminated Priya, the analytics lead, as she typed away at her keyboard.

Priya's eyebrows furrowed as she scrutinized a series of loan applications that had been flagged. "This doesn't add up," she murmured.

Avantika extended her arm over her shoulder. "What is the matter?"

Priya clarified, "We are observing anomalies in the system's risk assessments." "Subsequently, numerous applications that were identified as high-risk were approved without issue." Either an error was made by the system, or the decisions are being overridden by an individual.

Avantika experienced a shiver down her spine. "Is it possible for you to detect the overrides?"

Priya acknowledged. I will search through the records, but it will require a few hours.

Avantika's voice was firm as she replied, "Good." "Please inform me immediately upon discovering any new information."

Priya entered Avantika's office the following morning, holding a folder in her hand. Her countenance was oppressive.

She began by presenting the folder, stating, "You will not appreciate this."

Avantika accessed it and scanned the printouts of digital logs and audit traces. Her stomach churned as she recognized the user IDs associated with the overrides. They belonged to Ramesh's loyalists, who were mid-level administrators in the oversight committee.

Avantika's voice was icy as she declared, "They are sabotaging us from within." "This is deliberate; it is not incompetence."

Priya acknowledged. "The overrides are consistent with the grievances that Ramesh's team has been voicing regarding the system's dependability." It is an arrangement.

Avantika's thoughts ran wild. She was required to act with caution and urgency. Directly accusing Ramesh's team without substantial evidence would only serve to further undermine her credibility. She determined to accumulate additional evidence prior to initiating her action.

The following week, Avantika collaborated with Priya and Arjun to covertly monitor the system. They implemented a concealed monitoring mechanism that monitored each operation performed within the software. In the interim, Avantika remained composed during meetings with the oversight committee, responding to their pointed inquiries in a professional manner.

Nevertheless, Ramesh appeared to be more confident. At one meeting, he announced, "We have received a plethora of complaints from the branches," while simultaneously displaying a stack of printed emails. "The system is unreliable and is causing more harm than good." It is possible that it is time to reevaluate this experiment.

Avantika maintained an even gaze with him. "Mr. Bhardwaj, the data presents a different narrative." Processing times have improved substantially, and the majority of feedback has been favourable. We are addressing the concerns as they arise.

Ramesh's silence was more foreboding than his words, as he sneered but did not speak.

On a late evening, Priya entered Avantika's office with her laptop in hand, and the breakthrough occurred.

"We have them," she announced, her enthusiasm barely contained.

Avantika leaned forward as Priya pulled up the logs. The data demonstrated a distinct pattern of unauthorized overrides that originated from specific user accounts. Even more incriminating, the timestamps indicated that these actions occurred concurrently with committee meetings during which the system's reliability was investigated.

Avantika declared, her irises brimming with resolve, "This is it." "This is the evidence we require."

However, Avantika was aware that the presentation of the evidence necessitated meticulous preparation. She was unable to tolerate Ramesh and his cohorts manipulating the narrative to their advantage. She resolved to escalate the issue to the Chairman, Mr. Patel.

The meeting with Mr. Patel took place in his private office, a grand space adorned with framed awards and leather-bound volumes. Avantika meticulously organized the evidence, guiding him through the records and elucidating their implications.

Mr. Patel's expression darkened with each revelation as he listened attentively. When Avantika finished, he leaned back in his chair, his fingers steepled.

He ultimately stated, "This is a serious matter." "If accurate, it is not merely sabotage; it is a violation of trust and ethics."

Avantika responded, "I am cognizant of the gravity, sir." "However, I require your assistance in order to resolve this matter." They will place the responsibility on us and claim victimhood if we behave too aggressively.

Mr. Patel nodded. "Please leave it with me." In order to resolve this matter, I will organize an extraordinary board meeting. In the interim, please maintain the confidentiality of this matter. We are unable to inform them that we are aware of their actions.

The subsequent week was designated for the special board meeting. Avantika's team laboured tirelessly in the days preceding the event to prepare their case. Priya generated intricate visualizations of the data, while Arjun guaranteed that their presentation was immaculate.

The tension in the boardroom was tangible when the day arrived. Avantika was situated at the head of the table, with her team seated in close proximity to her. Ramesh and his allies maintained their unwavering confidence as they occupied their customary positions.

"I am grateful for your attendance at this unexpected meeting," Mr. Patel stated with a solemn demeanour.

"We have a significant issue to address, one that has a significant impact on the integrity of this institution."

He signalled for Avantika to commence. She deepened her inhalation and initiated her presentation by providing a summary of the objectives and results of the pilot phase. Then, she presented the board with the evidence of sabotage, guiding them through the records and establishing a connection between the actions of the oversight committee.

Her conclusion was met with silence in the chamber. Then, one of Ramesh's associates spoke up, his voice appearing defensive. "This is, at best, circumstantial." What methods can be employed to establish intent?

Arjun assumed responsibility. "The pattern is too consistent to be a coincidence." Additionally, the timing is in ideal harmony with the committee's concerns.

Ramesh attempted to regain control, his emotions visibly agitated. "This is a witch hunt." You are attempting to divert attention from the system's deficiencies.

Mr. Patel raised his hand, which effectively silenced him. "Enough." The evidence is self-evident. A comprehensive investigation will be conducted, and those who are discovered to be responsible will be subjected to repercussions.

Ramesh's composure has been compromised, and he exits the boardroom. Avantika observes him depart, aware that the conflict is not yet concluded, yet experiencing an unexpected surge of optimism. For the first time, she is not merely defending her vision; she is confronting those who attempt to undermine it.

Chapter 6:

The Reckoning

The special board meeting resulted in a rapid and vicious aftermath. Intrigue was abounding in the corridors of the National Progress Bank. Senior officials whispered in hushed tones, their conversations punctuated with stolen glimpses toward Ramesh's office. The once-unshakable General Manager of Operations now found himself in the midst of a tempest, his composure eroding with each passing day.

Avantika sat in her office, analysing the most recent performance metrics from the AI pilot branches. The project proceeded to surpass expectations in spite of the turbulence. Customer satisfaction ratings were at an all-time high, and processing times had decreased by 40%. The shadow of Ramesh's sabotage continued to loom enormous, but it was a validation for her efforts.

Her concentration was disrupted by a gentle knock at her door. Arjun entered the room with a laptop and a sense of urgency.

He began by placing the device on her desk and opening a succession of logs, "We have a problem." "It appears that Ramesh's camp is not yet complete." Examine these overrides.

Avantika leaned forward, scanning the data. The data indicated that the system's recommendations were unauthorizedly modified, which led to loan approvals that were questionable. Her mandible clenched as the implications began to sink in. "They are attempting to establish a paper trail that undermines the credibility of the system," she stated.

"Exactly," Arjun responded. "If this persists, they will assert that the AI is unreliable and employ it as a justification for terminating the project."

Avantika's thoughts ran wild. She was required to act with caution and urgency. She inquired, "Is it possible to isolate the accounts that are affected?"

"I have already completed it," Arjun stated, touching the screen. "We have identified the suspicious activity;

however, we must present it to Mr. Patel before Ramesh's team manipulates it."

Avantika assembled her core team in the analytics lab later that evening. The tense faces around the table were illuminated by the glow of multiple monitors in the dimly light room. Priya, the analytics manager, displayed a comprehensive dashboard that displayed the anomalies that had been flagged.

Priya clarified that these overrides are concentrated in two branches. "Both are overseen by individuals who have a close relationship with Ramesh."

Manish, the project manager, reclined in his chair with his arms crossed. "They are engaging in sloppy play, but they are playing dirty." This can be traced back to them.

Avantika acknowledged. "We must be methodical. Arjun, ensure that each instance is documented with user IDs and timestamps. "Priya, please create a report that emphasizes the discrepancies and their influence on the pilot's results."

"And what about Ramesh?" Manish inquired. "He will not remain silent as we construct a case against him."

Avantika's irises became inflexible. "Allow him to attempt." We are not merely defending this initiative; we are also revealing the corruption within this institution.

Avantika convened with Mr. Patel in his private office on the subsequent day. Avantika meticulously presented the findings, outlining the evidence of interference and its potential consequences.

The expression of Mr. Patel became more grave with each passing minute. He reclined in his chair, his fingertips trembling, as she concluded. "This is profoundly problematic," he stated. "Ramesh's actions are not only unethical; they pose a direct threat to the bank's credibility."

"What steps do you recommend we take, sir?" Avantika inquired.

Mr. Patel responded, "I will organize an emergency board meeting." "However, this must be approached with care." The evidence is damning; however, we cannot allow this to become a public spectacle.

The stately conference hall was the location for the emergency board meeting the following evening. A palpable tension supplanted the room's customary air of decorum. At one end of the table, Ramesh sat with a façade of self-assurance. Avantika was flanked by her main team on the other side.

Mr. Patel initiated the meeting with a succinct statement. "Ladies and gentlemen, we are present to discuss allegations of misconduct that have substantial implications for this institution." Ms. Agarwal, kindly present your findings.

Avantika stood, her voice unwavering despite the throbbing in her heart. She guided the board through the evidence, presenting logs, audit trails, and visualizations that illustrated the sabotage in a plain and concise manner. The room was filled with murmurs of outrage and astonishment as she spoke.

Ramesh's allies attempted to dispel the accusations after she had concluded.

Ramesh, evidently agitated, endeavoured to regain control. "This is a concerted assault on my reputation," he declared, his voice erupting.

Mr. Patel silenced him with an uplifted hand. "Enough." Compelling evidence is presented. There will be no tolerance for actions that compromise the integrity of this institution by this board. Accordingly, Ramesh, you are suspended until a comprehensive investigation has been conducted.

The decision's weight settled over the entire chamber, causing a moment of silence. Ramesh abruptly rose from his chair, it scratching against the floor. He dashed out without uttering a word, his departure a stark contrast to the confidence he had once exuded.

In the days that followed, the inquiry committee's investigation validated Avantika's findings. Safeguards were instituted to prevent future sabotage, and Ramesh's loyalists were reassigned. Avantika emerged as a respected and formidable leader, as the power dynamics within the bank began to shift.

However, the triumph was not without its drawbacks. Avantika contemplated the price of her victory as she stood on her office veranda, which provided a view of the Mumbai skyline, late one evening. The conflict had tested her resolve and strained her relationships, but it had also solidified her commitment to transforming the bank.

Avantika had emerged victorious in the equation. She was aware that the path ahead would necessitate an even larger level of fortitude. However, she permitted herself a moment to catch her breath, the city's lights serving as a reminder of the opportunities that were still within her grasp.

Chapter 7:

A New Frontline

Ramesh's suspension echoed through the bank's corridors. For some, it was a long-overdue realization; for others, it was a disturbing reminder of the fragility of their power structures. But for Avantika, it signified the commencement of a new chapter, one that was brimming with opportunities to reshape the institution and confront new challenges.

Stabilizing the oversight committee was Avantika's initial priority following Ramesh's departure. She recognized an opportunity to reassemble the team with individuals who prioritized innovation and merit as a result of the reassignment of a significant number of its members. She dedicated numerous hours to the evaluation of profiles, consultation with her core team, and meetings with potential candidates. By the end of the week, she had established the new oversight committee, composed of professionals with a reputation for integrity and a demonstrated track record.

During their inaugural meeting, Avantika declared, "This committee will serve as our foundation." "Our success is contingent upon a shared commitment to progress, transparency, and collaboration."

The team responded with enthusiasm, their energy a stark contrast to the tension that had previously characterized these gatherings.

In the interim, the AI pilot's accomplishments began to garner attention beyond the bank. The media began to cover the initiative in glowing terms, and industry analysts and competitors took note of the project's achievements. Avantika received an invitation to deliver a presentation at a prominent fintech conference in Mumbai, during which she provided her perspective on the system's evolution and its impact on the financial industry.

During her keynote address, she stated, "AI is not merely a tool." "It is a state of mind." It pertains to the reimagining of our approach to customer service, decision-making, and value creation. The rewards are transformative, despite the challenges of the voyage.

Thunderous applause greeted her speech, and several industry leaders approached her afterward, expressing interest in partnerships and collaborations.

Avantika returned to the bank with a reenergized sense of purpose and an expanding network of allies.

Nevertheless, her accomplishment was not universally embraced. Despite the recent turmoil, Neeta Sharma, the erstwhile Chief of Human Resources and a close ally of Ramesh, had been able to maintain her position. Neeta's resentment toward Avantika simmered beneath the surface, and she began discreetly rallying those who felt threatened by the bank's transformation.

One morning, Avantika's assistant entered her office with a look of apprehension. She placed a printed email on Avantika's desk, saying, "Ma'am, you should see this."

The email comprised accusations against Avantika, accusing her of prioritizing personal interests over the bank's welfare and mismanaging funds. It was sent anonymously to numerous senior executives and board members.

Avantika's chest constricted as she read the accusations. She was aware that they were unfounded; however, their timing and potential consequences were concerning. She murmured, "This is replete with Neeta's fingerprints."

Avantika resolved to confront the matter directly, rather than reacting reflexively. She invited external auditors to guarantee complete transparency and requested an internal audit of the pilot project's finances and operations. Additionally, she organized a meeting with the board to present the initiative's comprehensive financials, emphasizing its cost-effectiveness and favourable return on investment.

Avantika's meticulous preparation and composure during the meeting subdued her critics. The board categorically dismissed the allegations as unfounded, and Mr. Patel commended her for her proactive approach.

His eyes were fixated on Avantika as he stated, "This institution requires leaders who rise above pettiness and focus on the bigger picture." "You are serving as an example for all of us."

Avantika was aware that the fight for the bank's ethos was far from over, despite the victory. She collaborated closely with her team to establish policies that discouraged internal politics and emphasized accountability. One such initiative was the establishment of an anonymous feedback platform, which enabled employees of all ranks to express their apprehensions without fear of retribution.

Avantika instructed her team, "In order to establish trust, it is imperative that we provide individuals with a platform." This platform will assist us in the identification and resolution of issues prior to their escalation.

Initially met with scepticism, the platform quickly evolved into a valuable tool for promoting open communication within a matter of weeks. Avantika personally evaluated the feedback, addressing any apprehensions and instituting modifications as required.

Over several months, the board effectively completed the AI system's pilot phase and subsequently authorized its expansion to all branches. The project's success further solidified Avantika's status as a visionary leader, effectively subduing her critics.

One evening, while she was in her office reviewing the final implementation plan, Arjun entered with two cups of coffee. "Here's to the end of the pilot phase," he said, handing her a cup.

Avantika smiled, taking a sip. "And to the beginning of something bigger," she replied.

However, as they celebrated, a new obstacle loomed on the horizon. A competitor bank had declared its own AI initiative, asserting that it would surpass National Progress Bank's system. The announcement initiated the subsequent phase of Avantika's voyage, which would put her leadership, resilience, and vision to the ultimate test.

The chapter concludes with Avantika gazing out of her office window, the city lights reflecting her resolve. Although she was aware that the path ahead was uncertain, she was prepared to confront whatever lay ahead.

Chapter 8:

The Rivalry Unfolds

A rival bank, Stellar Finance, issued an announcement that caused significant disruptions in the financial sector. Their assertion that they would introduce an AI-driven system that would surpass the National Progress Bank's initiative was calculated, audacious, and unmistakably intended to obscure Avantika's accomplishments. It was the commencement of a high-stakes rivalry for Avantika, which would test her resilience and vision to unprecedented extents.

Avantika initially became aware of the announcement during her morning briefing. Arjun entered her office with a newspaper in his hand and an expression of bewilderment.

He inquired, depositing the paper on her desk, "Have you seen this?" The headline was "Stellar Finance Unveils Game-Changing AI Initiative." Immediately beneath it was a photograph of Raghav Mehta, the CEO of Stellar, shaking hands with a prominent technology collaborator.

Avantika's eyebrows furrowed as she perused the article's assertions. The system developed by Stellar was designed to provide predictive analytics for consumer behaviour, near-instant loan approvals, and integration with emerging fintech platforms. Everything that Avantika and her team had endeavoured to achieve was directly challenged by it.

Avantika's voice was steady but tinged with frustration as she stated, "This is deliberate." "They have been monitoring us and have strategically timed this event to disrupt our momentum."

Arjun acknowledged. "The technology partner they have enlisted is not a lightweight." If their assertions are accurate, they have the potential to acquire a substantial portion of the market.

Avantika reclined in her chair, her thoughts rushing. "It is imperative that we verify their assertions." Priya's team has the ability to evaluate their announcement and compare it to the capabilities of our system. We should ascertain the distinction between genuine information and marketing bluster.

Avantika's team laboured tirelessly over the next few days to scrutinize Steller's assertions. Priya supervised a task force that analysed public information regarding the rival system, while Arjun collaborated with external consultants to evaluate potential vulnerabilities. The results were both reassuring and alarming.

During a strategy meeting, Priya stated, "Their system is impressive on paper." "However, a significant number of their capabilities are still in the development stage." What they currently possess is being overpriced.

Manish further stated, "Their timeline for complete deployment is exceedingly ambitious and absurd." That is a substantial risk they are taking.

Avantika nodded in agreement, as she internalized the information. "They are relying on perception to attract customers and buy them time." It is imperative that we refute this narrative with empirical evidence and outcomes. We should concentrate on expediting our own implementation and demonstrating the system's effectiveness.

The media hysteria surrounding the rivalry intensified as the National Progress Bank prepared to counter Steller's challenge. The banking sector's implications were the subject of speculation among industry analysts, and opinion articles were a topic of debate regarding which system would establish the standard for AI-driven innovation. Avantika was suddenly propelled into the limelight, and her every action was closely monitored by both journalists and competitors.

Avantika consented to an exclusive interview with a prominent financial publication in order to address the increasing interest. The interview took place in a modern studio that provided a view of the Mumbai skyline, providing a vibrant setting for the discussion.

"Avantika," the interviewer initiated, "the industry is ablaze with discussion regarding your AI initiative and the recent announcement from Stellar Finance." What is your perspective on this rivalry?

Avantika's expression was composed and assured. "Competition is beneficial." It motivates us to enhance our customer service and innovate. At National Progress Bank, our primary objective is to generate tangible outcomes. We are dedicated to expanding upon the success of our system, which is already making a significant impact.

The interviewer continued to inquire. "Do you believe that your system is superior to Steller's?"

Avantika exercised meticulous judgment when selecting her words. "Each system has its own unique strengths." Our dedication to execution is what distinguishes us. We prioritize the delivery of quantifiable results, while others may prioritize promises.

Tensions within the bank began to resurface behind the scenes. Neeta Sharma, who was still resentful due to her diminished influence, viewed the rivalry as an opportunity to undermine Avantika. She insinuated doubts among middle management by disseminating rumours regarding the AI system's scalability.

Avantika was informed of Neeta's endeavours when a branch manager expressed apprehensions during a regional review meeting. "We have been informed that the system may encounter difficulties with increased transaction volumes," he stated with caution.

Avantika directly addressed the issue. "The system has undergone a comprehensive stress test." If you have any specific concerns, please communicate them through the appropriate channels, and we will promptly resolve them.

In the aftermath of the meeting, Avantika summoned Priya to her office. She stated, "I require a comprehensive examination of the system's performance metrics." "In addition, we should develop a communication strategy to mitigate any potential misinformation."

Stellar Finance increased their efforts as Avantika addressed internal challenges. They implemented an aggressive marketing campaign that capitalized on television advertisements, social media, and high-profile endorsements to establish themselves as the future of banking. The campaign included testimonials from early adopters who commended the system's quickness and convenience.

Avantika's team responded by emphasizing substance over flair. Detailed case studies were published to emphasize the AI system's influence on risk mitigation and consumer satisfaction. The studies bolstered the credibility of their claims by incorporating testimonials from loyal customers.

"Let Stellar focus on promises," Avantika told her team during a strategy session. "We'll focus on proof."

During the Global FinTech Summit in Singapore, the rivalry reached a climax. National Progress Bank and Stellar Finance were both invited to present their AI initiatives on the main stage, which presented a unique opportunity for direct comparison.

Avantika arrived at the summit with a presentation that was meticulously crafted. Her team had dedicated weeks to the revision of the visuals, the scripting of the narrative, and the rehearsal of the delivery. As she entered the stage, the entire audience's focus was directed toward her.

She began with a steady voice, "Good morning." "At National Progress Bank, we are of the opinion that innovation is not solely about technology; it is also about individuals." Today, I will discuss the ways in which our AI system is revolutionizing the banking industry by enhancing its speed, security, and inclusivity.

Her presentation featured compelling visuals, data-driven insights, and feedback of actual customers whose lives had been enhanced as a result of the system. The audience responded with enthusiastic applause, and several attendees approached her afterwards to convey their admiration.

Raghav Mehta was responsible for introducing Stellar Finance's system later that day. His presentation was both ambitious and professional; however, Avantika and her team observed inconsistencies while observing from the audience. Certain features appeared to be exaggerated, and certain claims lacked supporting data.

The two presentations were contrasted by industry analysts following the summit. The National Progress Bank's execution was praised as the more credible and impactful initiative, despite Steller's vision being praised. This sentiment was reflected in the headlines the following day, with one article stating, "National Progress Bank Leads the Way: Execution Triumphs Over Vision."

The rivalry with Stellar Finance marked a turning point for Avantika and her team. This encouraged them to accelerate their innovation, enhance their communication skills, and firmly establish themselves as industry leaders. But it also reinforced a critical lesson: success was not just about winning battles; it was about building a legacy.

While examining the accolades from the summit in her office that evening, Avantika experienced a revitalized sense of purpose. She was aware that she possessed the team, the vision, and the resilience to confront any upcoming obstacles, despite the fact that they were far from over.

Chapter 9:

Internal Fractures

Avantika's memory of the Global FinTech Summit's acclaim was still vivid upon her arrival at the National Progress Bank's headquarters. The accolades solidified the bank's reputation as a leader in AI innovation, but the future seemed filled with new complexities. One was internal fracture management, the other was external competition.

Early Monday morning, Avantika entered her office to the refreshing scent of freshly brewed coffee and the cool air conditioning that her assistant had set up. She noticed a notification from the anonymous feedback platform as she seated herself at her workstation. The notification read, "Management's emphasis on AI is leading to the neglect of traditional banking operations." Non-technical employees experience feelings of neglect and undervaluation.

The message tore at her. The AI initiative's rapid expansion had caused repercussions throughout the organization, despite its success. The showy new venture overshadowed the contributions of departments that were not directly involved with the project, resulting in a sense of alienation.

Avantika convened an unexpected meeting with her core staff. Arjun, Priya, and Manish arrived promptly, each bearing the burden of their respective departments' concerns.

"We are experiencing a morale issue," Avantika stated. People perceive our focus on AI as favouritism toward certain teams. It is fostering internal conflicts within the organization.

Arjun acknowledged. "I have encountered comparable feedback." Some of the branch managers believe that their operational challenges are being disregarded.

"And HR is inundated with grievances," Priya continued. "They are inundated with complaints regarding resource allocation and lack of recognition."

Avantika exhaled. "We must confront this issue directly." We should convene an all-hands meeting to address these concerns and establish a strategy for balancing priorities.
Hundreds of employees from branches throughout the nation participated virtually in the bank's largest conference room

for the all-hands meeting. A large screen projected Avantika's image behind her as she stood at the podium.

She initiated the conversation with a steady yet empathetic tone, "Good morning." "I would like to discuss a critical matter before we delve into the AI initiative announcements." In the past few weeks, I have received numerous inquiries regarding priorities and focus. I would like to assure you that your feedback is valued and that we are actively engaged in the process.

She then proceeded to provide a list of measures to guarantee that no department felt overlooked. These encompassed an open forum to address challenges at all levels of the organization, recognition initiatives for non-tech teams, and increased resources for branch-level operations. The atmosphere in the room had transformed from scepticism to cautious optimism by the conclusion of her speech.

But the organization's fractures were more profound than she had anticipated, despite her best efforts. Neeta Sharma, a perpetual opportunist, initiated the process of exploiting the discontent. She organized private meetings with employees who were disillusioned, portraying Avantika's leadership as elitist and divisive.

"This AI obsession is causing a rift within the bank," Neeta stated to a group of intermediate managers. "We have established this organization on the foundation of conventional banking principles that have endured for decades." Will we consent to its eradication?

Her rhetoric resonated with individuals who perceived themselves as overlooked by the digital revolution. Small enclaves of resistance began to emerge, and their voices became increasingly strident during internal discussions.

Avantika's core team laboured tirelessly to refute this narrative. Priya spearheaded a campaign that highlighted the triumphs of non-tech departments, demonstrating the advantages of integrating AI into traditional operations. Arjun collaborated with branch managers to resolve operational bottlenecks, ensuring they heard their voices.

However, the tension escalated during a senior leadership meeting. One of the regional leaders, a vocal opponent of the AI initiative, publicly challenged Avantika.

"With all due respect," he said, his tone cutting, "we are spending millions on this system while our rural branches are struggling to maintain basic infrastructure." What is the basis for your assertion?

Avantika took a deep breath and measured her response. "I comprehend your frustration, and I do not dismiss these apprehensions." However, this is not a binary choice. Future investments in AI will reap benefits across all sectors, including rural banking. Nevertheless, I am committed to tackling both immediate challenges and long-term goals.

Her words were met with a combination of unresolved tension and conviction, resulting in a moment of silence in the room.

In the interim, Stellar Finance's external pressure increased. Their aggressive marketing campaign persisted in creating significant ripples, and rumours circulated that they were recruiting employees from National Progress Bank. Avantika's team discovered that they had approached numerous mid-level employees with lucrative offers, raising concerns regarding retention and loyalty.

Avantika was aware that she had to take action with determination. She organized a strategy session with her core team to address both the internal fractures and the external threat.

"It is imperative that we reinforce our culture and demonstrate to our people the benefits of remaining here," she stated. "We should implement a retention strategy that encompasses a clear understanding of our objectives, competitive incentives, and career development opportunities."

Manish recommended the establishment of cross-departmental task forces to promote collaboration and diminish the gap between technical and non-technical teams. "Encouraging individuals to collaborate on common objectives will restore trust," he stated.

The team concurred, and the initiatives began to manifest within weeks. The retention plan effectively reduced the number of defections, as demonstrated by the gradual improvements in employee satisfaction surveys. Avantika's hands-on approach earned her the respect of many who had previously doubted her.

Amidst these endeavours, Avantika received an invitation to participate in a high-profile industry roundtable in Delhi. The future of finance was the subject of discussion at the event, which drew together CEOs and senior leaders from India's most prominent banks. Raghav Mehta, the charismatic CEO of Stellar Finance, was among the attendees.

The roundtable's discussions were fervent, encompassing a wide range of subjects, including emerging technologies and regulatory challenges. However, the most contentious discussion ensued when the moderator inquired about the impact of AI on the industry.

Raghav asserted with assurance, "AI is transformative." "However, it necessitates bold leadership and the readiness to take risks." Stellar Finance is dedicated to remaining at the forefront of the industry, even if it necessitates questioning conventional wisdom.

Avantika responded with the same level of conviction. "Leadership is not solely about risk-taking; it is also about achieving results." At National Progress Bank, we have demonstrated that innovation and tradition can coexist, resulting in value for both customers and employees.

Several attendees approached Avantika afterward to commend her poise and vision, and the audience erupted into applause. Even though the conversation with Raghav was civil, it emphasized the competitive tension between their institutions.

National Progress Bank had regained its equilibrium by the conclusion of the quarter. Stellar Finance's influence began to diminish as their overambitious timeline resulted in publicized setbacks, while the AI system's expansion proceeded without incident. Additionally, internal morale began to improve.

However, Avantika was aware that the conflict was far from over. One evening, as she was examining the progress reports in her office, her phone vibrated with a message from an unknown number. The message was as follows:

"Success breeds enemies. Stay vigilant."

Avantika continued to gaze at the screen, her thoughts churning. The message was both cryptic and unambiguous: the obstacles that lay ahead would necessitate her utmost fortitude and ingenuity.

The chapter concludes with Avantika standing by her office window, the city lights reflecting the victories she has already achieved and the conflicts that lie ahead.

Chapter 10:

The Silent War

The cryptic message that Avantika received remained in her mind for an extended period of time after she had read it. It was a warning that she could not afford to disregard, despite its nebulous but foreboding meaning. Her instincts informed her that it was not merely paranoia; success frequently attracted threats from competitors, internal adversaries, or unseen forces.

Avantika was resolute in her commitment to safeguarding the AI project's operations and her professional reputation, determined not to be caught off guard. A strategy that was both meticulous and deliberate was required in the upcoming weeks.

Internal Security Measures

Avantika initiated a private meeting with Arjun, Priya, and Manish in her office as one of her initial actions.

She began, "The message I received may be unfounded; however, we cannot afford to take any chances."

I require a comprehensive audit of our system's security, including both digital and operational components. If there is a vulnerable link, we must identify it before anyone else does.

Arjun acknowledged. "We will conduct penetration tests on the AI's backend and strengthen access protocols." Additionally, I will examine user activity records for any discrepancies.

Avantika continued, "Priya, begin reviewing the data pipeline." I would like to be informed immediately if any inputs have been tampered with or results have been flagged.

"Understood," Priya replied. "I will ensure that my team prioritizes this."

Manish's arms were lying on the table as he leaned forward. "What about the branches?" The sabotage may be occurring offline if Stellar Finance or any other competitor has embedded an individual inside.

"That is a valid point," Avantika responded. "We should broaden the audit to encompass operational workflows at pilot branches." Ensure that we are monitoring employee behaviour without causing them to feel like they are being singled out.

The team's renewed sense of vigilance was a testament to their confidence in Avantika's leadership, as evidenced by their shared determination upon leaving the meeting.

Unexpected Alliances

Avantika received an unexpected call from a senior executive at Stellar Finance two weeks into the security audit. Steller's Head of Innovation, Aniket Roy, was a well-known figure at industry events. His voice was composed, yet it was tinged with a sense of urgency.

"Avantika," he initiated, "I will proceed directly to the point." I have reason to suspect that an individual is directing their attention toward both of our financial institutions. This isn't just competition; it's sabotage."

Avantika's grasp on the phone became increasingly firm. "Why do you believe that?"

We have observed data irregularities and attempts to infiltrate our systems," Aniket clarified. "It is excessively coordinated to be a mere coincidence." I have a suspicion that a third party is attempting to exploit vulnerabilities in order to position us against each other.

Avantika's thoughts ran wild. Stellar had been her most formidable adversary; however, Aniket's assertions were authentic.

"If this is accurate, we cannot afford to disregard it," she stated. "Let us exchange information in a discreet manner." We will track down the common thread if it exists.

The call concluded with a tentative accord, an alliance that was not established on the basis of trust but rather on the basis of mutual necessity.

The Discovery

Arjun entered Avantika's office with a menacing visage one week later. "You must view this," he stated, positioning his laptop on her desk.

A sequence of log entries from the AI system's backend was displayed on the screen. Unauthorized access attempts had been detected in numerous branches, all of which were initiated from external IP addresses that were concealed by VPNs. However, Avantika was particularly intrigued by the timing.

She said, her voice low, "These breaches are consistent with Steller's reported issues."

Arjun acknowledged. "It is not a mere coincidence." Whoever is conducting this activity is adept at manipulating financial systems. They are focusing on decision-making algorithms and exploiting their vulnerabilities.

Avantika reclined in her chair, the burden of the situation resting on her shoulders. "We must escalate this matter to the board and Mr. Patel." This is no longer solely about us; it poses a hazard to the entire industry.

The Boardroom Revelation

The emergency board meeting was conducted in the bank's high-security conference room.

Avantika meticulously detailed her findings, elucidating the coordinated nature of the attacks and their potential implications.

The expression on Mr. Patel's face darkened as he listened. "This is not merely sabotage; it is cyber warfare if these breaches are as highly sophisticated as you are implying."

A erstwhile cybersecurity expert, one of the board members, intervened. "Regulatory authorities and law enforcement must be engaged." This degree of coordination implies the presence of a structured group, potentially even state-sponsored actors.

As the board deliberated on the subsequent actions, the room was filled with a sense of urgency. Avantika's leadership earned her silent respect from even her harshest detractors, as her calm, authoritative presence kept the discussion focused.

A Race Against Time

Avantika's team worked tirelessly to fortify the AI system and monitor the assailants as the investigation progressed. Stellar Finance's findings, which were also shared by Aniket Roy, indicated comparable patterns of intrusion. The two banks jointly recognized a shared thread: the assailants were exploiting vulnerabilities in third-party vendor software that was utilized by both institutions.

Avantika promptly initiated a comprehensive examination of vendor contracts and security protocols. "We must address the gaps in our supply chain immediately if they are being exploited," she advised her team.

In the interim, Priya discovered a disturbing detail. Customer data was the target of some of the assailants' activities. "Our reputation could be irreparably damaged if they intend to disclose this information," she cautioned.

Avantika responded promptly. She released a public statement that recognized the threat and delineated the measures being implemented to safeguard customers. Regulators and the media commended her transparency, which bolstered the National Progress Bank's reputation as a forward-thinking and responsible institution.

The Finale

The joint investigation yielded results after weeks of unwavering effort. The assailants were identified as a cybersecurity firm that was operating illegally in Eastern Europe. Their objective was to capitalize on the resulting disarray and undermine prominent financial institutions.

The firm's operations were raided by law enforcement agencies, which were notified by the institutions. National Progress Bank and Stellar Finance were recognized for their cooperation and diligence in the aftermath of the removal, which garnered global attention.

A New Chapter

Avantika's status as a leader was not only established within her organization but also throughout the industry as a result of the crisis. Additionally, the experience imparted to her valuable lessons regarding the significance of collaboration and the constantly changing nature of hazards in the digital era.

One evening, while she was in her office perusing the final report on the investigation, her phone vibrated with a message from Aniket Roy:

"For what it's worth, you handled this with grace. Let's keep our rivalry clean from here on out."

Avantika's thoughts were already turning to the next challenge as she faintly smiled. The silent war had been successfully concluded; however, the struggle for the future of banking was far from over.

Chapter 11:

The Aftermath and the Vision Ahead

The takedown of the rogue cybersecurity firm was a resounding success, and the banking industry collectively breathed a sigh of relief. The media lauded National Progress Bank and Stellar Finance for their cooperation, a rare moment of unity in an otherwise cutthroat industry. However, for Avantika, the victory brought as many concerns as it did accolades.

Regaining Stability

The immediate aftermath of the crisis required Avantika's attention on multiple fronts. The incident has left customers and employees with lingering concerns, despite the fact that the attackers have been neutralized. Although the bank's reputation was unblemished, it was necessary to reestablish trust.

Avantika's first priority was to address customer concerns. She initiated a series of initiatives with the objective of restoring confidence, such as providing regular updates on improved security measures and providing a 24/7 customer helpline. Community engagement events were conducted by the bank's branches to conduct direct interactions with customers and resolve their inquiries.

During a televised press conference, Avantika stated, "We are dedicated to establishing your trust on a daily basis." Her calm demeanour and clear communication reassured stakeholders, and feedback from customers began to reveal a positive shift.

On an internal level, Avantika prioritized morale. She held town hall meetings with employees across all levels, acknowledging their efforts during the crisis and delineating the steps being taken to fortify the bank's defences.

"This was a test of our fortitude," she informed them. "And we succeeded." But we must remain vigilant and united as we progress forward."

Unfinished Business

Despite the progress, Avantika knew the internal fractures within the bank had not magically healed. The crisis had revealed the weaknesses in organizational cohesion, and

Neeta Sharma continued to incite dissatisfaction among specific factions.

Avantika confronted these obstacles during a leadership meeting.

"The cyberattack has demonstrated that external threats are not the sole risks we encounter," she stated. "Internal unity is equally important." From now on, our leadership's primary focus will be on building a culture of trust, accountability, and collaboration."

She suggested a variety of strategies, such as a rotational leadership program, to promote cross-departmental understanding and dismantle silos. The program was met with a variety of responses; however, its implementation was guaranteed by Avantika's conviction and the board's support.

She stated, "It is imperative that we collaborate as a single entity." "Our survival depends on it."

A New Partnership

As National Progress Bank stabilized, Avantika's thoughts turned to the future. The potential for alliances, even among competitors, was demonstrated to her through her collaboration with Stellar Finance during the crisis. She proposed a groundbreaking initiative, which was inspired by this experience: a consortium of banks to share resources and intelligence on cybersecurity.

The "Secure Bank Alliance" proposal was initially greeted with scepticism. Many questioned the feasibility of competitors working together on such a sensitive issue. Nevertheless, Avantika's persuasive abilities and the undeniable necessity of collective defence progressively won over key stakeholders.

At an industry roundtable, she contended that cyber hazards are not selective. "If we collaborate, we can stay ahead of attackers and ensure the safety of our customers."

The alliance acquired momentum as a result of the signing of numerous prominent banks as founding members.

The initiative not only improved cybersecurity but also established Avantika as a visionary leader in the industry.

Personal Reflection

Avantika found herself contemplating her journey in the midst of the whirlwind of professional accomplishments. She was put to the test in ways she had never anticipated by the obstacles she encountered, including internal sabotage, industry rivalries, and cyberattacks. However, they had also developed her into a leader who flourished in high-pressure situations.

Avantika's thoughts turned to her family one evening as she perched on her balcony, which provided a view of the Mumbai skyline. Her parents, who had imparted in her the values of perseverance and hard work, frequently reminded her to maintain a sense of stability. She made a mental note to visit them soon, knowing she owed much of her success to their unwavering support.

Additionally, she contemplated her core staff. Arjun, Priya, and Manish had been her pillars of strength throughout the journey. Their dedication and proficiency had been indispensable in surmounting each challenge.

"Leadership is never a solo journey," she pondered, raising a toast to the city lights.

The Next Frontier

As the months passed, the Secure Bank Alliance became a model for industry collaboration, attracting interest from international banks and regulators. National Progress Bank's AI initiative continued to thrive, extending its capabilities to encompass personalized financial planning and predictive analytics for customer requirements.

However, new challenges hovered on the horizon. The rapid pace of technological advancement has resulted in ethical dilemmas, particularly in the areas of data privacy and automation's impact on employment. Avantika was aware that these matters would determine the subsequent phase of her leadership.

During a strategic planning session with her core team, she addressed these challenges candidly.

She stated, "The future of banking is not solely about technology." "The objective is to strike a balance between innovation and accountability. "We need to lead with empathy and ensure that our progress benefits everyone, not just a select few."

The team brainstormed ideas for ethical frameworks, customer education programs, and reskilling initiatives for employees whose roles were evolving. Avantika's vision was clear: to create a bank that was not only innovative but also inclusive.

The chapter concludes.

As Avantika walked through the bank's headquarters one evening, she noticed the buzz of activity around her. Employees were collaborating, customers were being served efficiently, and the AI system's monitors displayed real-time insights. It was a scene that reflected the resilience and progress of an institution that had weathered innumerable storms.

Avantika paused for a moment, taking it all in. She felt a profound sense of satisfaction, despite the fact that the journey was far from over, as she had contributed to the bank's progress toward a more promising future.

The chapter closes with Avantika standing at the threshold of her office, ready to face whatever lay ahead with the same determination that had carried her this far.

Chapter 12:

Winds of Change

Anticipation permeated the atmosphere of the National Progress Bank's headquarters. The AI initiative had achieved unprecedented success, receiving recognition on both a national and international scale.

Avantika led the Secure Bank Alliance, strengthening the industry's defences against cyber threats. However, Avantika could sense an undercurrent of transformation, a subtle yet potent shift in the banking landscape that required her unwavering focus amidst these accomplishments.

A New Opportunity

Avantika's assistant entered her office on a brisk Monday morning, carrying an embossed envelope. "Ma'am, this has been delivered to you," she announced, depositing it on the desk.

Avantika discovered an invitation to the Global Banking Leaders Forum in Zurich in the envelope she had opened. This exclusive event is attended by CEOs and thought leaders who are influencing the future of finance. Avantika's vision was profoundly aligned with the forum's theme, "Reimagining Banking in the Digital Age."

One session caught her attention as she reviewed the agenda: a panel discussion on the ethical implications of AI in finance. Avantika was aware that this was her chance to confront a matter that was particularly meaningful to her. She promptly accepted the invitation and initiated the event preparations with her core team.

"This is not solely about representing the bank," she informed Arjun, Priya, and Manish during a brainstorming session. "The objective is to shape the global discourse on responsible innovation."

Internal Challenges Resurface

Avantika's momentum was at risk of being derailed by internal obstacles as she prepared for the forum. Neeta Sharma, encouraged by a group of dissatisfied employees, began to discreetly advocate for modifications to the leadership structure. Her rhetoric was concentrated on the

"Preservation of traditional banking values" and the "restoration of balance" to an institution that she stated was excessively preoccupied with technology.

Avantika became aware of Neeta's manoeuvrers through whispers in the corridors and anonymous tips from allies within the bank. Instead of confronting Neeta directly, Avantika elected to address the underlying causes of her dissatisfaction. She initiated an internal campaign known as "Banking Together" with the objective of uniting employees from various departments and commemorating their shared accomplishments.

The campaign included team-building exercises, town hall meetings, and an awards program that acknowledged the contributions of all levels of the organization. It was a resounding triumph, as employees expressed a renewed sense of pride in the bank's direction and their work.

Neeta's efforts to garner support were undermined by the campaign's positive influence, which caused her influence to diminish. Nevertheless, Avantika maintained her prudence, as she was aware that internal politics would never be entirely eradicated.

The Zurich Forum

Avantika appeared on a modern, streamlined stage in Zurich on the day of the Global Banking Leaders Forum, where she was surrounded by industry leaders. The panel discussion on AI ethics was the event's crowning achievement, attracting a captivated audience that was anxious to hear a variety of viewpoints.

Avantika's opening remarks set the tone for the discussion. "As bankers and technologists," she said, "we must remember that every algorithm, every data point, represents real people. Fairness, transparency, and inclusion must be the primary focus of our innovations.

The panellists engaged in a vibrant debate as a result of the profound resonance of her insights. Some argued for the implementation of more stringent regulations to regulate AI, while others favoured the industry's self-regulation. Avantika's balanced approach, which advocated for a combination of technological advancement and ethical frameworks, garnered her widespread admiration.

Avantika was approached by executives from prominent banks, fintech companies, and regulatory authorities during the subsequent networking sessions. Her status as a global thought leader was further solidified by the numerous expressions of interest in collaborating on initiatives inspired by the Secure Bank Alliance.

A New Rival Emerges

After returning to Mumbai, Avantika's attention was redirected to the bank's operations. Nevertheless, it was not long before a new obstacle arose. Horizon Bank, a financial institution that is rapidly expanding, has unveiled a groundbreaking blockchain-based platform that is designed to revolutionize cross-border transactions.

The industry was impacted by the announcement. Horizon's blockchain platform assured unparalleled security and efficiency in global commerce, in contrast to National Progress Bank's AI initiatives, which prioritized customer-centric solutions. Analysts began to speculate about the potential of Avantika's leadership to withstand this new tide of competition.

Avantika assembled her core team to deliberate on the implications.

Arjun declared, "Blockchain is a game-changer." "If Horizon fulfils their commitments, it has the potential to revolutionize the international banking industry."

Priya further stated, "We must assess the extent to which blockchain aligns with our long-term strategy." It would be an error to disregard this.

Avantika concurred. "We should establish a task force to investigate the potential applications of blockchain in our ecosystem." We have pioneered the field of AI; it is now time to broaden our perspectives.

The Blockchain Task Force

The task force, which was composed of experts in finance, technology, and operations, initiated its work by pinpointing critical areas in which blockchain could provide value. These encompassed digital identity verification, supply chain financing, and cross-border payments. The board was presented with the team's findings, as well as a proposition to pilot a blockchain-based solution in partnership with a prominent technology firm.

Avantika's vision for the pilot was clear: "This isn't about following trends; it's about solving real problems. Our customers deserve solutions that are fast, secure, and trustworthy."

The proposition was approved by the board, and the pilot was implemented in a limited number of markets. The initial results were encouraging, as clients expressed satisfaction with the reduced operational costs and speedier transaction times.

Navigating Ethical Dilemmas

As the blockchain pilot gathered momentum, ethical concerns emerged. Compliance, data privacy, and accountability were all raised as concerns regarding blockchain's decentralized nature. Avantika, who was cognizant of the AI initiative's lessons, guaranteed that the pilot complied with rigorous ethical standards.

She established an oversight committee to oversee the pilot's progress and mitigate potential hazards. The committee was comprised of representatives from the legal, compliance, and customer advocacy departments, which guaranteed a comprehensive decision-making process.

Avantika highlighted during a committee meeting that "innovation without ethics is a recipe for disaster." "We must lead with integrity, even if it means moving at a slower pace than our competitors."

The Chapter Concludes

National Progress Bank had effectively integrated blockchain technology into its operations by the end of the year, further solidifying its status as a pioneer in the banking sector. The bank was able to attract new customers and strengthen existing relationships by leveraging the power of AI and blockchain to position itself at the forefront of digital transformation.

In the midst of the bank's bustling headquarters, Avantika contemplated the voyage that had so far taken her there. Her resolve was put to the test by each obstacle, which ranged from internal politics to industry rivalries. Nevertheless, she had grown stronger with each challenge, driven by a steadfast dedication to excellence and a well-defined vision.

Avantika gazes out at the Mumbai skyline, a symbol of boundless potential, as the chapter concludes. She was aware that the journey was far from over, even though the winds of change had carried her far. She was prepared to embrace the challenges and opportunities that lay ahead, as the future beckoned.

Chapter 13:

Confronting the Past

National Progress Bank's blockchain initiative was a huge triumph, propelling the institution into a new category of innovation-driven banks. Avantika's leadership established a precedent in the financial sector, resulting in her invitations to international think tanks and accolades. However, an ineffable sensation persisted as she progressed; the foundation she had laboriously constructed was at risk of being destroyed by loose ends from her past.

A Sudden Disruption

Avantika arrived at the bank on a chilly morning in December to discover her assistant standing at the entrance of her office, her expression emaciated.

"Ma'am, there is an issue," the assistant informed her, passing her a folder. Emails and memos that had been leaked were included within. The contents indicated that specific financial irregularities had been concealed during the implementation of a legacy system years ago.

Avantika's pulse plummeted as she examined the documents. Although she was not directly involved in the decision-making process, her predecessor's name was prominently mentioned, as well as the names of a few crucial senior managers who still held influential positions within the bank.

She inquired, "From where did this originate?"

"A whistleblower who remains anonymous." It is also present in the media. They are currently in the process of compiling narratives.

Avantika's thoughts ran wild. This was not merely a public relations crisis; it was a potential scandal that had the potential to undermine the bank's credibility and undermine trust in its leadership.

Damage Control Begins

Avantika promptly organized an emergency meeting with the bank's legal counsel and her core team. The room was tense as she described the situation.

Avantika stated with conviction, "Transparency is imperative." "The situation will only deteriorate if we attempt to conceal it." Priya, commence the process of verifying the authenticity of these documents. Arjun, evaluate any potential operational or legal hazards that may arise. Manish, collaborate with HR to anticipate potential staff reactions.

Manish inquired, "And the media?"

The expression of Avantika became more stern. "We will not release a statement until we have collected all the necessary information." The last thing we need is to appear unprepared or evasive.

Unearthing the Truth

Priya's team laboured tirelessly for the next 48 hours to verify the contents of the documents and trace their origin. In the interim, Arjun discovered that the irregularities were the result of an outdated procurement contract that was associated with a failed IT project. Even though no laws had been explicitly violated, the absence of oversight and ethical violations presented a damning picture.

Late into the night, Avantika meticulously reviewed the results in her office. These revelations demonstrated a pattern of prioritizing short-term gains over long-term accountability, despite the fact that her predecessor had been praised as a transformative leader. Even worse, the bank's leadership team continued to include some of the senior managers who were implicated in the memos.

Facing the Board

In order to resolve the crisis, the board organized an emergency session. The room was fraught with tension as Avantika presented the findings.

She commenced, "These events transpired prior to my tenure; however, I am fully accountable for their consequences in my capacity as the institution's current leader." Transparency, accountability, and action are our only paths forward."

The board members listened attentively as Avantika delineated her proposed measures:

1. Commissioning an independent audit to review the bank's practices during the period in question.

2. Placing the implicated senior managers on administrative leave pending further investigation.

3. Establishing a compliance task force to ensure such lapses could never happen again.

4. Hosting an open forum with employees to address their concerns and reinforce the bank's commitment to ethics.

Mr. Patel, the chairman, leaned back in his chair, his expression thoughtful. "This is a bold approach, Avantika. It'll ruffle feathers, but it's the right thing to do. You have my full support."

A Reckoning Within

The independent audit's announcement caused ripples of shock throughout the bank. The managers who were implicated in the incident responded with a combination of resignation and outrage as employees murmured in the hallways. Ever the opportunist, Neeta Sharma capitalized on the opportunity to sow additional discord.

Neeta informed a group of middle managers that Avantika is attempting to rewrite history at our expense. "She is exploiting this scandal to fortify her authority."

Avantika, who was cognizant of Neeta's mischief, declined to engage in trivial disputes. Rather, she concentrated on guiding the bank through the tempest. Her open forums with employees were candid and sincere, enabling her to reaffirm her vision for the bank and address their concerns.

"Errors were committed," she informed them, "but we must not permit the past to dictate our future." We will work together to restore trust and guarantee that this institution is more robust than ever.

Media Scrutiny

The media's coverage of the scandal intensified as the independent audit progressed. Avantika's leadership was the subject of scrutiny, and headlines speculated about the potential consequences. However, her decision to confront the issue directly earned her respect in specific circles.

A prominent financial correspondent composed the following:

"Avantika Agarwal's handling of this crisis is a masterclass in accountability." She has opted for transparency and action, whereas others may have attempted to avoid responsibility. She is currently establishing a new standard for leadership in Indian banking, but the outcome of her venture will only be determined in the future.

The Audit Report

The independent audit's findings were published three months later. The authenticity of the disclosed documents was verified by the report, which also identified systemic governance issues within the bank during the period in question. Nevertheless, it also commended the reforms that were implemented under Avantika's leadership, highlighting substantial enhancements in compliance and oversight.

Avantika conducted a press conference to elaborate on the results.

"The audit has revealed uncomfortable truths about our history," she stated, her voice remaining steady. "However, it has also demonstrated the extent of our progress." I am grateful to each and every employee who has dedicated their time and effort to the restoration of this institution. We are not yet finished with our journey; however, today, we are taking another stride toward establishing the trust of our clients.

A Fresh Start

Avantika shifted her focus to the future after the audit was completed. A new leadership team was appointed to replace those implicated in the scandal, and the compliance task force's recommendations were implemented bank-wide. Neeta Sharma, unable to adjust to the shifting tides, discreetly resigned, her influence reduced to the whispers of a bygone era.

Avantika emerged from the experience with an unprecedented sense of resolve. She was aware that leadership was not solely about celebrating successes; it also involved confronting failures with courage and integrity. Walking through the bank's bustling headquarters, she experienced a revitalized sense of purpose. The past had been reckoned with, and the future awaited.

The chapter ends with Avantika standing by her office window, the city lights reflecting the resilience of an institution that had weathered the storm. The road ahead was still uncertain, but for the first time in months, she felt truly ready to face it.

Chapter 14:

The Road to Transformation

National Progress Bank initiated a new chapter of recovery and regeneration months after the independent audit and the repercussions of the financial irregularities scandal. Avantika had guided the institution through one of its most challenging periods with unparalleled fortitude, and the bank was gradually regaining the confidence of its stakeholders, clients, and employees.

Nevertheless, she was aware that merely reconstructing was insufficient; the bank must undergo a transformation, surpassing expectations and redefining its role in the rapidly changing financial ecosystem.

A Vision for the Future

Avantika addressed the senior leadership team of the bank from the top of the boardroom table. Department heads, regional administrators, and members of the recently established compliance task force were present in the room.

The title of her presentation was displayed on a screen behind her:

"Vision 2030: National Progress Bank's Blueprint for Sustainable Growth."

Avantika began, her voice unwavering and confident, "We have come a long way." "However, the banking industry is evolving at an unprecedented pace." To remain pertinent and resilient, we need to think beyond traditional metrics. We must be the driving force behind the advancement of sustainability, inclusion, and innovation.

Her presentation delineated three fundamental components of the bank's transformation:

1. **Digital Acceleration:** The expansion of AI and blockchain initiatives to encompass new areas, including micro-lending and financial literacy tools for marginalized communities.

2. **Sustainable Banking:** The implementation of green financing programs and the commitment to environmentally responsible practices throughout all operations.

3. **Customer Empowerment:** Redesigning products and services to prioritize customer education, transparency, and personalization.

As Avantika concluded her presentation, the room was filled with a combination of exhilaration and apprehension. The ambitious objectives she had established were intimidating; however, her vision was so clear and unwavering that there was little space for uncertainty.

"This is our opportunity to redefine the definition of a bank," she stated. "We should not merely satisfy expectations; we should surpass them."

Building the Digital Frontier

The establishment of a specialized task force known as "Digital Horizon" was a direct result of Avantika's emphasis on digital acceleration. Arjun was appointed as its leader, with Priya serving as its analytics head. The team's objective was to explore state-of-the-art technologies and incorporate them into the bank's operations.

Micro-lending was the primary focus of the inaugural Digital Horizon initiative. Avantika had been a proponent of financial inclusion for a considerable period of time, and she perceived micro-lending as a means of empowering small businesses and individuals who are frequently disregarded by conventional banking.

During the task force's inaugural meeting, Avantika stated, "Our objective is to ensure that credit is accessible to all." "But accessibility isn't enough. It is essential that we guarantee that it is both sustainable and advantageous to our clients.

The team created a credit assessment instrument that is AI-driven and specifically designed for micro-loans. In order to assess creditworthiness, the instrument implemented alternative data sources, including utility payments and social behaviour patterns. The approval rates increased by 25% and default rates remained low in the initial trials conducted in rural branches, which demonstrated promising results.

Green Financing Takes Root

Concurrently, the bank's dedication to sustainable banking began to manifest. Avantika collaborated with environmental organizations to establish a green financing initiative that was designed to assist businesses in their transition to environmentally favorable practices. The program provided companies that invested in renewable energy, sustainable agriculture, and waste reduction technologies with preferential loan terms.

Avantika was featured on a prominent business news channel in order to advertise the initiative. She emphasized the importance of institutions in the fight against climate change during the interview.

"As financial institutions, we have a responsibility to drive change," she said. "Each loan and investment we approve has the potential to influence the environment." At National Progress Bank, we are dedicated to ensuring that the impact is beneficial.

The program rapidly acquired momentum, with dozens of businesses enrolling within the first few months. The initiative was lauded by analysts as a bold step toward aligning profitability with purpose.

Reimagining Customer Experience

The bank's customer experience strategy was entirely restructured as a result of Avantika's emphasis on customer empowerment. Manish was recruited to supervise a cross-functional team that was responsible for the redesign of the bank's products and services.

One of the team's first achievements was the launch of a financial literacy app dubbed "MyProgress." The application offered consumers personalized insights, budgeting tools, and educational resources to assist them in making well-informed financial decisions. Additionally, it included an AI-powered chatbot that was capable of providing personalized recommendations and responding to inquiries.

Customers, media representatives, and industry executives attended the app's launch event. Avantika's speech at the event captured the essence of the initiative:

"The purpose of banking is to empower, not to intimidate." We are empowering our customers with the knowledge and control necessary to make informed decisions that contribute to their financial objectives through MyProgress.

The application's popularity exceeded expectations, with more than one million downloads in the span of six months. The user-friendly interface and practical insights were the most notable features that customers emphasized in their feedback.

Navigating Challenges

As the bank's transformation initiatives acquired momentum, obstacles arose. The initiatives' ambitious scope resulted in occasional delays and employee burnout, as the resources were strained to the limit. Avantika's vision was criticized by critics for being excessively expansive, as they feared that it could endanger the bank's stability.

Avantika prioritized transparent communication in order to address these concerns. She provided employees with consistent updates, recognizing the challenges and underscoring the significance of their work.

During a town hall meeting, she informed her team that "every great transformation comes with growing pains." "Nevertheless, it is important to bear in mind that we are not merely altering procedures; we are also altering the lives of individuals." We should maintain our concentration and provide mutual encouragement throughout this endeavour.

Avantika ensured that employees felt valued and supported by implementing wellness programs and flexible work policies in order to mitigate fatigue. The measures were instrumental in maintaining momentum and enhancing morale.

A Symbol of Progress

National Progress Bank had made substantial progress in its transformation by the year's conclusion. The AI-driven micro-lending initiative has expanded nationwide, offering financial opportunities to thousands of underprivileged individuals. The bank was recognized as a leader in sustainable banking on a global scale as a result of the green financing program. The MyProgress app continued to cultivate deeper engagement and loyalty by empowering customers.

Avantika gazed at the city lights from the rooftop terrace of the bank's headquarters one evening. The institution she had devoted her life to transforming was symbolized by the skyline, which represented its potential and resilience. Despite the numerous obstacles she encountered during her voyage, each obstacle served to fortify her resolve.

Her phone vibrated with a message from Mr. Patel as she contemplated the future directions:

"Congratulations on all you've achieved this year. The board is proud of your leadership."

Avantika smiled, her thoughts already shifting to the future. She was aware that with the appropriate team and vision, anything was feasible, despite the fact that the journey to transformation was far from complete.

The chapter ends with Avantika standing under the night sky, a symbol of hope and determination in a world of constant change.

Chapter 15:

A Turning Point in Leadership

National Progress Bank experienced a series of key developments during the first quarter of the year. Avantika then shifted her focus to positioning the institution as a leader in global finance after stabilizing the bank's operations and restoring trust. Yet, as she sought to elevate the bank's profile, she found herself grappling with the complexities of leadership in an increasingly volatile industry.

The Push for Global Expansion

At a board meeting in early February, Avantika's aspiration to expand internationally was the centre of attention. She highlighted her aspiration to establish a presence in Southeast Asia, a region that is currently undergoing rapid economic development and digital transformation.

Avantika articulated with assurance that Southeast Asia presents an immense opportunity for financial services.

"Our proficiency in artificial intelligence (AI) and blockchain technology can satisfy unmet requirements in these markets, with a particular emphasis on digital payments and micro-lending."

A vigorous debate was initiated by the proposal. The hazards of entering unfamiliar territories were the subject of concern for certain board members, who cited cultural differences and regulatory challenges. The move was perceived by others as a logical progression for a bank that had already demonstrated its innovation capabilities.

The chairman, Mr. Patel, made a decisive statement. "The opportunity is too substantial to be disregarded." We should proceed with caution, beginning with a feasibility study to identify potential partners and target markets.

Avantika's resolve was unwavering as she nodded. "I will personally supervise the investigation and guarantee that we conduct it with the utmost care."

Navigating Internal Resistance

Although the board's approval was a significant milestone, Avantika encountered internal opposition. The international expansion was perceived by certain senior managers as a diversion from the consolidation of the bank's domestic operations.

During a town hall meeting, a regional head voiced these concerns.

"Ma'am, are we not overextending ourselves?" Our employees are still in the process of recuperating from the obstacles they faced last year.

Avantika responded to the inquiry with her customary Candor. "Your apprehensions are legitimate, and I concur with your dedication to assisting our team." This is the reason for the gradual and meticulous management of this expansion. Domestic operations will continue to be our primary focus, and we will guarantee that our resources are allocated effectively.

Many employees expressed renewed confidence in her leadership as a result of the honesty of her response.

The Feasibility Study

Promising opportunities in the Philippines, Vietnam, and Indonesia were identified during the three-month feasibility study. In these markets, there was a substantial unbanked population, a growing demand for digital services, and supportive regulatory environments. Potential local partners, such as fintech startups and regional institutions, were also identified in the study.

Avantika presented the findings at a subsequent board meeting, along with a comprehensive roadmap for entering these markets. The strategy comprised the following:

1. Forming joint ventures with local partners to navigate regulatory landscapes.

2. The beginning of pilot programs that concentrate on digital wallets and micro-lending

3. Establishing a specialized staff to supervise international operations.

The plan was unequivocally approved by the board, and Avantika's vision began to manifest.

The Challenge of Retaining Talent

The retention of top talent presented a new challenge for Avantika as the international expansion acquired momentum. Competing offers from global institutions threatened to poach key members of her team, as the financial sector's rapid evolution had made skilled professionals highly sought after.

In order to resolve this issue, Avantika collaborated with HR to create a comprehensive retention strategy. The plan encompassed initiatives to cultivate a sense of belonging, competitive compensation packages, and career development opportunities.

One such initiative was the establishment of a "Leadership Academy," which was intended to prepare high-potential employees for future leadership positions. Avantika delivered an inspiring keynote address during the academy's inaugural session.

She stated, "Leadership is not about titles or positions." "It's about taking ownership, driving change, and making a difference. Each of you has the capacity to influence the future of this institution.

A Crisis in the Making

A crisis emerged that threatened to impede the bank's progress just as the international expansion was taking off. A wave of negative publicity and regulatory scrutiny was initiated when sensitive customer information was exposed by a data breach at one of the bank's fintech partners.

In order to resolve the crisis, Avantika organized an emergency meeting with her leadership team.

"It is imperative that we act with urgency and resolution," she stated. "Arjun, prioritize the investigation of the breach and the security of our systems." Priya, compile an exhaustive report for regulators. Manish, guarantee that our customer support team is adequately prepared to address inquiries.

A public statement was issued by the bank within days, acknowledging the breach and delineating the measures being taken to safeguard customers. Avantika's proactive approach and transparency were commended by stakeholders; however, she was aware that the crisis had exposed vulnerabilities that required attention.

The Road to Recovery

The data exposure necessitated an exhaustive assessment of the bank's cybersecurity protocols. Avantika was responsible for the development of sophisticated threat detection systems and the reinforcement of partnerships with prominent cybersecurity organizations. Additionally, she initiated a consumer awareness campaign to inform users about the importance of safeguarding their personal information.

During a town hall meeting, she informed employees that "trust is the foundation of our business."

"It is imperative that we take all necessary measures to protect it."

The bank's immediate response and long-term strategies were instrumental in restoring trust among regulators and customers. The institution was once again on solid ground by the conclusion of the quarter.

A Milestone Achievement

Avantika's aspiration for international expansion became a reality despite the obstacles. The bank successfully implemented pilot programs in Vietnam and Indonesia, providing digital payment solutions and micro-loans that rapidly gained popularity. The bank's strategy was validated by the pilots' success, which paved the way for future expansion.

Avantika addressed employees and stakeholders at the bank's headquarters during a celebratory event.

"This achievement is a testament to our innovation and resilience," she stated. "We have collectively demonstrated that National Progress Bank is capable of competing on a global scale while adhering to our principles."

The Chapter Ends

Avantika acknowledged that the voyage had been a combination of triumph and adversity as she contemplated the previous year. Her leadership was put to the test in unexpected ways by the challenges, but they also fortified her resolve.

She observed the city lights from the window of her office, which served as a testament to the bank's boundless potential and enduring spirit. Avantika was prepared to lead with the same fortitude and vision that had propelled her to this point, despite the fact that the road ahead would undoubtedly present new obstacles.

The chapter closes with Avantika reaffirming her commitment to the bank's mission, her eyes set firmly on the future.

Chapter 16:

Forging Alliances, Bridging Gaps

Avantika's leadership was widely recognized as a result of the success of National Progress Bank's international expansion; however, it also increased the complexity of her responsibilities. The difficulties of navigating diverse regulatory frameworks, cultural nuances, and economic volatility became more evident as the institution delved deeper into global markets. In addition to innovation, Avantika was aware that the subsequent phase of growth would necessitate a steadfast dedication to establishing connections both within and beyond the organization, as well as strategic alliances.

The Dawn of Strategic Alliances

In the Southeast Asian markets where the bank had established a presence, Avantika's initial objective was to fortify partnerships with local competitors. She acknowledged the importance of collaboration in achieving sustainable growth and contacted prominent fintech companies, microfinance institutions, and regional banks.

Avantika facilitated a partnership with a prominent fintech company that specializes in digital wallets in Indonesia. National Progress Bank was able to integrate its payment solutions with the fintech's platform as a result of the collaboration, which significantly increased market penetration.

During the press conference that announced the partnership, Avantika emphasized the significance of mutual development.

She stated, "This collaboration is a testament to the potential we can achieve when we combine our strengths." "We are not only improving financial access but also enabling communities to flourish."

Avantika's team collaborated with a government-backed microfinance institution in Vietnam to establish a collaborative initiative that was designed to provide assistance to small and medium-sized enterprises (SMEs). The program was recognized by local policymakers for its provision of financial literacy seminars and low-interest loans.

Internal Integration

The integration of the new ventures with the bank's extant framework became a critical focus as international operations expanded. The task force, which was convened by Avantika and commanded by Priya, was established to guarantee that domestic and international operations were in perfect harmony.

Avantika reiterated during the task force's inaugural meeting that "we are not constructing silos." "Our capacity to function as a single, unified entity, utilizing insights and expertise that transcend national boundaries, is our greatest asset."

In order to facilitate real-time communication and decision-making across markets, the task force implemented a centralized data platform. Additionally, they implemented cultural exchange programs to facilitate the exchange of knowledge and the cultivation of mutual understanding among employees from various regions.

One such exchange sent Nguyen, a young Vietnamese finance officer, to the bank's headquarters in Mumbai. Nguyen reflected on his experience, stating, "This opportunity has demonstrated to me the possibility of coexistence between tradition and innovation." It is a source of inspiration to be a part of a vision that surpasses national boundaries.

Bridging generational gaps

Avantika encountered an increasing obstacle at the bank's headquarters: reconciling the generational gap in the workforce. The newer generation of employees, motivated by innovation and purpose, frequently encountered conflicts with the seasoned professionals who prioritized stability and time-tested practices.

Avantika directly addressed the issue during an employee town hall.

She stated, "Each viewpoint in this room is valuable." "Our distinctions are not a source of weakness, but rather a source of strength." We can establish a culture that values tradition while also embracing progress by exchanging knowledge.

Avantika implemented an initiative known as "Connect" to encourage collaboration. This initiative involves the pairing of junior employees with seasoned mentors in a structured program. The initiative promoted reverse mentorship, in which junior employees shared their technological expertise while learning leadership and strategic thinking from their mentors.

The program's influence was immediate. A digital instrument that simplified loan applications was developed by Rohan, a junior analyst with a strong technical background, in collaboration with Meera, a seasoned corporate banking professional. Their collaboration not only improved efficiency but also fortified the feeling of camaraderie among generations.

Navigating geopolitical risks

The bank's strategic considerations were inevitably influenced by geopolitical hazards as global operations expanded. The micro-lending program of the bank in the Philippines was at risk of disruption due to an abrupt shift in government policy. Avantika responded by assembling a team of experts in regulatory affairs and diplomacy to resolve the matter.

Additionally, she personally contacted local officials to underscore the bank's dedication to community development and ethical practices. In a meeting with the country's finance minister, she effectively negotiated a compromise that enabled the program to continue with minor adjustments as a result of her efforts.

Avantika contemplated the meeting's conclusion.

"Leadership is not solely about numbers; it is about relationships." The most critical investment we can make is in the development of trust.

A Renewed Commitment to Sustainability

Avantika's vision for the bank encompassed a profound dedication to sustainability, in addition to financial growth. The success of the green financing initiative motivated her to introduce a new program known as "Sustainable Progress."

The program concentrated on three key areas:

1. **Green Bonds:** The issuance of bonds to finance sustainable infrastructure and renewable energy initiatives.

2. **Carbon Neutrality:** The bank's carbon footprint will be reduced by transitioning to renewable energy and implementing eco-friendly practices across all branches.

3. **Community Engagement:** Collaborating with environmental organizations to inform communities about sustainability.

Avantika expressed her enthusiasm for the initiative during a global finance summit.

She stated, "We are obligated to influence a more favourable future as stewards of capital." "Sustainability is an absolute necessity; it is not an option."

The program was met with extensive acclaim, attracting investors who were similarly dedicated to the bank's environmental and social governance (ESG) principles.

The Chapter Ends

National Progress Bank had accomplished milestones that were considered unattainable only a few years ago by the year's conclusion. Its sustainability initiatives established a new industry standard, its workforce became more cohesive, and its alliances in Southeast Asia flourished.

Avantika contemplated the journey they had undertaken together as she stood before her leadership team during a year-end gathering.

"This year has demonstrated that progress is not a linear process," she stated. "It is a collection of triumphs, challenges, and lessons." We have collectively demonstrated that we are capable of accomplishing anything with resilience, collaboration, and vision.

The chapter concludes with Avantika gazing towards the night sky, a representation of the boundless potential that awaits both the bank and the communities it serves.

Chapter 17:

Balancing Innovation and Tradition

National Progress Bank encountered novel opportunities and challenges with the commencement of a new fiscal year. The institution had established itself as a global innovator under Avantika's leadership; however, the rapidity of its transformation had caused some stakeholders to become increasingly uneasy. The defining theme of this phase in Avantika's journey was the delicate balance between the preservation of the bank's legacy and the drive for modernization.

The Roots of Tradition

As the bank expanded its global footprint and rolled out cutting-edge solutions, its older clientele—those who had been with the institution for decades—began voicing concerns. The abrupt transition to digital platforms was perceived as alienating by a significant number of individuals. Avantika's team received a significant amount of feedback that emphasized the perceived erosion of the bank's fundamental values, the loss of personal interaction, and the frustrations associated with automated services.

Avantika, acknowledging the significance of these sentiments, embarked on a listening tour of branches that were renowned for their loyal, long-standing customer base. She encountered Mr. Deshmukh, an 82-year-old retired professor who had been a customer for more than 50 years, during one of these visits to a branch in Pune.

"I understand the need for progress," Mr. Deshmukh said, "but I miss the days when I could walk into the branch, sit with a manager, and discuss my needs without feeling rushed or replaced by a machine."

Avantika responded with empathy. "The foundation of this bank is your loyalty and trust." We are dedicated to achieving a harmonious equilibrium that acknowledges our past while welcoming the future.

This exchange inspired Avantika to rethink the bank's strategy for customer engagement.

Human-Centric Banking

Avantika initiated an initiative known as "Heritage Connect" to resolve these concerns by integrating technology with personalized service. The program encompassed the following:

1. **Improved Branch Experiences:** The introduction of designated Relationship Officers in branches to assist senior customers and those who are less acquainted with digital tools.

2. **Community Banking Events:** Organizing consistent gatherings that provide customers with the opportunity to engage with bank staff, participate in financial seminars, and offer feedback.

3. **Hybrid Service Models:** Ensuring flexibility for a variety of preferences by allowing customers to switch between digital and traditional service methods.

Heritage Connect was accompanied by an emotive advertising campaign that tells the stories of intergenerational banking relationships. One ad showcased a grandfather teaching his grandson about saving money, supported by both a traditional passbook and a digital app. The campaign struck a chord, revitalizing the bank's image among its legacy customers.

Innovation Unveiled

Innovation remained the cornerstone of Avantika's development strategy, despite her emphasis on preserving the bank's heritage. The successful pilot programs in Southeast Asia facilitated the introduction of "Progress Global," a collection of digital financial tools that were specifically developed for emerging markets.

Progress Global featured:

- **Digital Lending:** Streamlined micro-loan approvals using AI-driven assessments.

- **Mobile Wallets:** Secure and user-friendly platforms tailored for cash-reliant economies.

- **Localized Features:** Customization options to meet cultural and regulatory nuances.

The launch event in Jakarta attracted widespread media attention, with Avantika delivering a keynote address that emphasized the program's potential to drive financial inclusion.

She stated, "Progress is not about imposing solutions that are universally applicable." "The objective is to equip each community with the resources necessary to flourish by comprehending the distinctive requirements of each community."

The bank's dedication to innovation as a force for good was further solidified by the program's initial success in Vietnam and Indonesia.

Internal Crossroads

Internal dynamics became more intricate as external progress flourished. While initiatives such as "Connect" attempted to resolve the generational divide within the workforce, it continued to manifest in various ways. While seasoned professionals favoured a measured approach, younger employees advocated for the rapid adoption of emergent technologies.

Two department heads—Rahul, a tech-savvy millennial, and Meera, a veteran with 30 years of experience at the bank—engaged in a contentious debate regarding mechanization in loan processing during a leadership workshop. This moment was critical.

Rahul contended that automation expedites approvals and minimizes errors. "Why continue to rely on manual reviews when technology is capable of performing them more efficiently?"

Meera responded, "Banking is not solely about efficiency; it is also about relationships." The trust that is established through human interaction cannot be replaced by automated decisions.

Avantika intervened, emphasizing the necessity of equilibrium. "Both viewpoints are legitimate." Our objective should be to utilize technology in a manner that promotes human discernment, rather than supplanting it. Before scaling, we should evaluate the impact of a hybrid model through a pilot program.

The compromise promoted mutual respect and promoted more collaborative decision-making.

A Test of Resilience

In the midst of these developments, a natural calamity struck the Philippines, causing widespread devastation and disrupting the bank's operations in the area. Avantika's leadership and the institution's resilience were put to the test during the crisis.

Avantika promptly activated the bank's disaster response framework, with a focus on the protection of customers and employees. Additionally, she authorized emergency funds to assist communities that were impacted and collaborated with local organizations to offer assistance.

Avantika stated during a press briefing that our responsibilities extend beyond financial services. "It is incumbent upon us to provide support to these communities during their most difficult periods."

The bank's prompt and compassionate response was met with widespread acclaim, further solidifying its status as a socially responsible institution.

Leadership Beyond Borders

The experiences of the year deepened Avantika's understanding of leadership. She was invited to deliver a keynote address at the World Economic Forum in Davos, where she spoke on the theme of "Banking for a Better Tomorrow."

Her speech highlighted the significance of maintaining a balance between innovation and empathy, progress and tradition, and growth and sustainability.

"Leadership is about finding harmony in complexity," she said. "It's about making decisions that honour the past, address the present, and shape a future where everyone can prosper."

Avantika's status as a global financial industry thought leader was solidified by the standing ovation she received during the speech.

The Chapter Ends

National Progress Bank was situated at the nexus of tradition and innovation as the year concluded, under the leadership of a leader who recognized the significance of both. Although the institution's voyage was far from complete, its foundation had never been more robust.

In her office, Avantika reviewed a handwritten note from Mr. Deshmukh, the retired professor she had met months earlier.

"Thank you for listening to us. The bank feels like home again."

Avantika placed the note on her desk with a smile, serving as a reminder of the enduring influence of empathy and connection.

The chapter concludes with Avantika gazing at the city lights, her mind brimming with ideas for the future, and her heart anchored in the values that had guided her thus far.

Chapter 18:

The Legacy Blueprint

As an institution that is synonymous with innovation, community trust, and resilience, the National Progress Bank began its subsequent fiscal year. Avantika's leadership had not only guided the bank through challenging periods, but it had also redefined its ethos, thereby establishing it as a model for progressive banking. However, as the bank achieved new heights, Avantika found herself contemplating the perennial issue of legacy—how to guarantee that the institution's values and vision would persist beyond her tenure.

A Visionary Summit

In order to resolve this issue, Avantika organized a unique leadership summit that included senior executives, board members, and a select group of emerging leaders within the organization. The objective was clear: to establish a comprehensive strategy for the bank's future.

Avantika declared in her inaugural address, "We have accomplished extraordinary milestones." "However, genuine success is not solely determined by our current accomplishments." The objective is to establish the foundation for tomorrow. We have the opportunity to establish the legacy of the National Progress Bank at this summit.

Workshops, strategy sessions, and keynote speeches from industry executives were all part of the summit. Priya conducted a session that concentrated on the influence of AI and blockchain on the future of finance. Manish led another initiative that aimed to prepare a workforce for the challenges of the upcoming decade.

The discussions were fundamentally driven by a shared dedication to innovation, inclusivity, and sustainability. Participants collaborated in cross-functional teams to develop proposals that addressed critical areas, including ethical banking practices, consumer empowerment, and digital transformation.

Codifying Values

Avantika presented the "Legacy Values Framework" as one of the summit's outcomes, a document that encapsulates the fundamental principles that had influenced the bank's development.

The framework outlined five pillars:

1. Customer-Centricity: Prioritizing customer needs and ensuring accessibility for all demographics.

2. Innovation with Integrity: Leveraging technology responsibly to enhance services without compromising ethics.

3. Sustainability: Committing to environmentally and socially responsible practices.

4. Employee Empowerment: Fostering a culture of collaboration, growth, and well-being.

5. Community Impact: Strengthening ties with the communities served and contributing to their development.

In a plenary session, Avantika elaborated on the significance of the framework.

She stated, "These values are not merely words on a page." "They are the bedrock of our identity." They will provide us with guidance as we negotiate the intricacies of the future.

Mentoring the Next Generation.

Avantika's emphasis on legacy encompassed the development of the next generation of leaders. She personally mentored a group of high-potential employees, sharing insights from her journey and encouraging them to think critically about the challenges and opportunities ahead.

During a mentorship session, Kavya, a young analyst with a passion for sustainability, proposed a daring concept.

"What if we established a Green Innovation Lab within the bank?" Kavya recommended. "It could serve as a collaborative environment in which employees and external collaborators collaborate on initiatives that generate both financial and environmental benefits."

Avantika was impressed. "That's exactly the kind of forward-thinking we need," she said. "Let's pilot this idea and see where it takes us."

The Green Innovation Lab rapidly acquired momentum, establishing itself as a central hub for initiatives such as carbon-neutral operations and renewable energy financing. The bank recognized Kavya as one of its rising stars due to her leadership in the initiative.

Strengthening community ties

In the interim, Avantika reiterated the bank's dedication to community engagement. She initiated the "Progress Together" initiative, which was designed to stimulate economic development in underprivileged regions.

The program encompassed the following:

- Financial Literacy Camps: Conducting educational sessions on digital banking, credit, and savings for rural populations.

- Entrepreneurship Grants: Offering mentorship and seed funding to entrepreneurs and small businesses.

- Infrastructure Development: Collaborating with local administrations to enhance the accessibility of banking services.

In Uttar Pradesh, Avantika encountered beneficiaries of the program during a visit to a village. Ramesh, an entrepreneur, recounted how a modest grant had facilitated the establishment of his dairy business.

Ramesh stated, "This grant has significantly altered my life." "It is not solely about the financial gain; it is about the faith that someone had in me."

Avantika reiterated the bank's dedication to the improvement of communities, moved by his narrative.

She stated, "Your success is our success." "By working together, we can establish a more promising future for all."

Navigating New Challenges

Despite the bank's progress in innovation and community impact, it encountered new obstacles. Economic uncertainties, increasing competition, and changing regulations necessitated consistent adaptability and vigilance.

Avantika met these obstacles with a proactive approach. She established a "Future Readiness Task Force" to anticipate and confront emerging trends. The task force engaged in scenario planning exercises, which involved the examination of potential scenarios, including the impact of artificial intelligence on the workforce and the emergence of decentralized finance.

Avantika informed the task force that our longevity will be contingent upon our capacity to adjust. "Let us guarantee that we are not merely responding to change but rather directing it."

The Chapter Ends

Avantika convened her leadership team for a contemplative session as the fiscal year concluded. They collaborated to evaluate the year's accomplishments, obstacles, and insights.

Avantika stated, "We have established a foundation for a legacy that will endure beyond our lifetimes." "However, our work is not yet complete." We should persist in our efforts to challenge norms, press boundaries, and uphold our principles.

The session concluded with a standing ovation, which served as a testament to the respect and reverence that Avantika had garnered.

Avantika experienced a profound sense of fulfilment as she stood in her office, gazing at the city lights, later that evening. The journey had been difficult, but each obstacle had provided an opportunity for personal development. She was certain that the foundation she had established would endure, despite the uncertainty of the future.

Avantika concludes the chapter by composing a message to her team that reads, "I am grateful for your support of this vision." We are not merely constructing a bank; we are also establishing a legacy.

Chapter 19:

The Culmination of a Vision

The grand atrium of National Progress Bank's headquarters was buzzing with anticipation. An event that had become synonymous with the bank's transformative journey, the Annual Leadership Summit was attended by employees, board members, industry leaders, and representatives from communities across the country. Nevertheless, this year was particularly significant, as it represented the completion of Avantika's vision, a moment of reflection and commemoration of her exceptional leadership.

A Grand Opening

A resounding ovation greeted Avantika as she entered the stage. Her quiet confidence was the result of years of navigating challenges, inspiring teams, and leading with purpose. Her presence conveyed this confidence.

She began, her voice steady and resonant, "Today is not just a celebration of milestones." "This is a testament to the potential we have when we unite under a common vision." National Progress Bank has consistently been more than a financial institution. We are builders of dreams, enablers of progress, and champions of resilience."

Avantika delivered a retrospective of the bank's history, emphasizing its most significant accomplishments, as the audience began to settle.

- Expansion into five international markets, with flagship initiatives in micro-lending and digital payments transforming lives.

- Industry-leading sustainability programs, including the issuance of $1 billion in green bonds

- A 40% increase in customer satisfaction ratings, driven by the "Heritage Connect" program and personalized services.

- Recognition as one of the top employers in the financial sector, thanks to initiatives like the "Leadership Academy" and "People First" programs.

Each statistic drew applause, a reflection of the pride shared by everyone in the room.

A Decade of Change

Avantika's thoughts veered to the journey that had led her to this juncture as she spoke. She assumed leadership of a bank that was contending with internal conflict, external obstacles, and a swiftly evolving industry environment a decade ago. The transformation had been challenging, necessitating a steadfast commitment to the power of collaboration, unremitting effort, and the ability to make difficult decisions.

The whistleblower crisis, which challenged the bank's integrity; the cyberattack, which necessitated resilience; and the natural calamity in the Philippines, which emphasized the significance of community engagement, were the turning points that she recalled. A sturdier, more adaptable institution was formed as a result of the bank's unwavering determination to confront each challenge.

However, the accomplishments were not solely hers. Avantika's leadership philosophy was founded on the principle of empowering others, and she had assembled a team of exceptional individuals. Collectively, they had established a culture that prioritized accountability, empathy, and innovation.

The Announcement

As the applause subsided, Avantika's expression grew contemplative. She stepped forward, her voice tinged with emotion.

She stated, "Leadership is a process." "The key is to recognize when to take the lead and when to allow others to take the lead." I am filled with a sense of immense gratitude and pride as I stand before you today, but I am also aware that it is time to embark on a new chapter.

The room fell silent as Avantika disclosed her intention to step down from her position as CEO at the conclusion of the fiscal year. The audience listened attentively as she articulated her reasoning.

The decision is not one of retreat, but rather of renewal, she stated. "National Progress Bank is on the brink of even greater accomplishments, and I am of the opinion that it is time for new perspectives to advance our vision."

Her remarks were greeted with a combination of admiration and surprise. Although numerous individuals experienced the gravity of her declaration, they also comprehended her dedication to the institution's legacy.

Passing the torch

Avantika worked assiduously in the months that followed to guarantee a smooth transition. She worked with the board to select her successor, focusing on candidates who exemplified the bank's values and exhibited a dedication to inclusivity and innovation.

Priya Sharma's appointment as CEO was broadly well received. Priya, a dependable member of Avantika's leadership team, had played a critical role in the bank's sustainability and digital transformation initiatives. Her appointment represented progress and continuity.

Avantika addressed the audience during a ceremonial handover ceremony.

She stated, "Leadership is the act of constructing bridges." "The objective is to establish opportunities for others to assume leadership roles." Priya is the optimal candidate to lead National Progress Bank into its next chapter due to her dedication, vision, and integrity.

Priya's reply was sincere. "Avantika, your leadership has served as a source of inspiration for all of us." I am privileged to continue the legacy you have established and to guide this institution with the same passion and purpose.

A Personal Reflection

Avantika paused to contemplate her voyage as her final day as CEO approached. She revisited the branches that had been instrumental in her professional development, reestablishing connections with the employees and consumers whose narratives had served as sources of inspiration for her.

The rural branch in Uttar Pradesh was one of her visits, where she had encountered Ramesh, the dairy entrepreneur. The village's development was facilitated by the success of his business, which employed numerous local labourers.

Ramesh informed her, "Your confidence in me has transformed everything." "The bank's assistance provided me with a future that I had never considered feasible." Avantika's eyes were filled with tears. "The genuine evaluation of our efforts is your success." I am grateful for your reminder of the rationale behind our actions.

The Farewell

Avantika was surprised with a celebration at the headquarters on her final day. The atrium was filled with employees who held banners and signs that read, "Thank You, Avantika!" and "Forever Our Leader."

During her farewell speech, Avantika expressed her gratitude.

She stated, "This is not the end." "It marks the establishment of a new chapter for all of us." The honour of my life has been the journey that we have embarked on together. I depart with the assurance that National Progress Bank will persist in its success, guided by the principles we have established in collaboration.

Cheers and a standing ovation greeted her remarks. She was surrounded by colleagues as she descended the stage, and many of them shared intimate anecdotes about the impact of her leadership on their lives.

A New Chapter

Avantika transitioned into a new role as an advisor and mentor in the weeks that proceeded, dedicating her time to supporting emerging leaders and contributing to the global conversation on ethical leadership and sustainable banking.

National Progress Bank continued to thrive under Priya's leadership. Avantika's vision's enduring influence was evidenced by the institution's unwavering dedication to sustainability, innovation, and community impact.

The Chapter Ends

Avantika experienced a profound sense of satisfaction as she sat on her veranda, which provided a view of the Mumbai skyline. Her journey was characterized by growth, triumphs, and challenges, but it was ultimately a journey of purpose.

A concluding note is written by Avantika in her journal, which concludes the chapter:

"Leadership is not about the destination; it is about the journey we undertake together." It is about the legacy we leave behind, the values we uphold, and the lives we influence. "This is not the conclusion; it is a continuation of the creations we have made."

Chapter 20:

The Legacy Lives On

The optimism that emanated from the corridors of the National Progress Bank's iconic headquarters in Mumbai appeared to be mirrored by the bright sunlight that streamed through its windows. The bank's centennial celebration commemorated one hundred years of growth, innovation, and service. Avantika Agarwal, a revered figure in global banking, sat among the dignitaries in the audience, her presence a reminder of the institution's transformative journey.

A Moment of Reflection

A compilation was displayed on a large screen at the commencement of the ceremony, which detailed the bank's historical milestones. The images transitioned from black-and-white photographs of its modest origins to vibrant snippets of its innovative initiatives in AI, blockchain, and sustainability. Avantika's tenure was prominently featured, showcasing her critical role in guiding the bank through its most innovative and challenging periods.

Avantika experienced a sensation of nostalgia while seated. She reflected on the day she entered the bank as a young manager, brimming with ambition and ideas. She had never anticipated the extent of their mutual success or the personal development she would undergo during the process.

A New Era

The keynote address was delivered by Priya Sharma, the current CEO and Avantika's protégé. She commenced by recognizing the contributions of previous leaders, with a particular emphasis on Avantika.

Priya's voice was brimming with emotion as she stated, "It is a privilege to serve as the leader of this institution." "We are supported by the shoulders of giants, and Avantika Agarwal is the most prominent." Her unwavering dedication to excellence, resilience, and vision has left an indelible impression on this organization and on all of us.

Avantika experienced a surge of pride as the audience erupted in applause. Priya's words emphasized the enduring influence of the values she had imparted.

The Unveiling

The Avantika Agarwal Centre for Innovation and Leadership, a cutting-edge facility that is committed to cultivating creativity and preparing future leaders, was the centrepiece of the celebration. The centre boasted state-of-the-art financial technology laboratories, collaboration spaces for cross-functional teams, and a mentorship program for emerging talent.

Avantika was invited to the stage as the curtain fell to disclose the centre's name in bold letters. She approached the podium amid a standing ovation, her heart overflowing with joy.

She initiated, "This moment is not about me." "It pertains to the numerous individuals who were convinced of a vision that was greater than their own." This centre is a testament to our shared dedication to empowering the next generation to lead with compassion and courage, embracing change, and challenging boundaries.

The essence of the bank's mission was encapsulated by her words, which resonated profoundly.

The People Behind the Progress

Additionally, the centennial commemoration included stories from employees, customers, and partners whose lives had been significantly impacted by the bank. They shared anecdotes of opportunities realized and challenges surmounted one by one.

Ramesh, a dairy entrepreneur from Uttar Pradesh, discussed the impact of a modest loan on his business and community.

"This bank didn't just give me a loan; it gave me hope," he said. "Today, my business employs 50 people, and we're able to support our families and neighbours. That's the power of believing in someone."

Kavya, who is currently the director of the Green Innovation Lab, shared an additional narrative regarding the groundbreaking initiatives that her team had initiated, including the implementation of carbon-neutral operations and renewable energy financing.

"This institution empowers us to dream big and act boldly," she said. "It's a privilege to be part of a legacy that prioritizes progress for people and the planet."

Avantika's Quiet Legacy

As the celebration progressed, Avantika began to contemplate her own legacy. She was always of the opinion that leadership was about facilitating the success of others, and the thriving institution that was in front of her only served to reinforce that conviction.

Priya approached Avantika later that evening as the festivities concluded.

"I hope we've made you proud," Priya said.

Avantika's expression was amiable. "More than you can conceive." This vision has been advanced beyond my wildest expectations by you and the team. The future is in the capable hands of exceptional individuals.

A Vision for the Future

The following morning, Avantika visited the Avantika Agarwal Centre for Innovation and Leadership. She was awed by the energy and creativity that radiated from every corner as she strolled through its corridors. The enduring power of purpose-driven leadership was exemplified by the enthusiasm of young professionals who worked on initiatives ranging from digital inclusion to sustainable finance.

She discovered a group in one room that was engaged in the process of devising strategies to integrate AI with renewable energy financing. In another, a team deliberated on methods for increasing financial access in underserved regions. She observed the future being influenced by passionate individuals in every direction.

A young employee approached her with apprehension. "Ms. Agarwal, may I ask you something?"

Avantika responded with a positive tone, "Certainly."

"What is the most significant lesson you have acquired regarding leadership?"

Avantika thought for a moment before responding. "Leadership is about service," she said. It's about putting others before yourself, listening more than you speak, and staying true to your values no matter how difficult the journey becomes."

The young employee nodded, clearly moved by her words.

The Chapter Ends.

Avantika returned to her residence as the sun set over Mumbai, her emotions overflowing with gratitude and contentment. She composed the final entry in her journal while sitting by her window.

"A century ago, National Progress Bank was founded with a simple mission: to serve. Today, it stands as a testament to what is possible when we lead with purpose, innovate with integrity, and stay rooted in our communities. My journey with this institution has been the honour of a lifetime, but its story is far from over. The next chapters will be written by those who dare to dream, who embrace change, and who believe in the power of progress. And I will always be cheering them on."

The final chapter concludes with Avantika gazing at the city lights, a symbol of the limitless possibilities that await those who follow in her footsteps and the enduring legacy she has established.

Epilogue:

A Legacy Beyond Measure

The Mumbai skyline was illuminated by the soft tints of dawn, and the morning was serene. Avantika Agarwal sat in her garden, consuming chai, her gaze adrift to the horizon. Although she was officially retired from her position as CEO of the National Progress Bank, her days were still packed with purpose. Writing, mentoring new leaders, and accepting invitations to speak at global forums continued to consume her time. However, as she contemplated her voyage, she experienced an immense sense of satisfaction—a legacy that was not solely based on her accomplishments but also on the lives she had impacted.

A New Chapter

Two years had passed since Avantika's departure, and the bank continued to thrive under Priya Sharma's leadership. The institution's mission of financial inclusion was furthered by its expansion into ten international markets. The Green

Innovation Lab and "Progress Together," which were implemented during Avantika's tenure, had become industry standards.

Avantika maintained her relationship with the bank as an advisor, offering assistance when required while allowing Priya to operate independently. Their relationship had evolved into a friendship that was rooted in mutual respect and a common vision.

During one of their encounters, Priya had stated, "You have constructed something that is timeless, Avantika." "Your legacy should not be limited to the bank; it should encompass the principles that will serve as a beacon for future generations."

Mentoring the Future

Avantika's dedication to cultivating talent transcended the finance sector. A platform dedicated to mentoring young professionals across sectors, the "Agarwal Foundation for Leadership and Innovation" was established by her. The foundation provided seminars, scholarships, and one-on-one mentorship programs.

Aarti, a social entrepreneur and one of her mentees, shared how the foundation had altered her perspective.

During a foundation event, Aarti stated, "I believed that leadership was solely about making decisions before I met Avantika ma'am." "She instilled in me the notion that genuine leadership is the act of enabling others to discover their own voice."

These encounters reignited Avantika's conviction regarding mentorship's effectiveness. Every conversation with a protégé was an opportunity for her to impart the knowledge she had acquired.

The World Stage

Avantika's influence had expanded beyond the confines of banking. She became a highly sought-after speaker at global summits, as her perspectives on innovation, sustainability, and ethical leadership resonated with audiences across the globe.

She delivered a keynote address at the United Nations Leadership Forum regarding the function of financial institutions in confronting global challenges. Her speech, "Banking on Humanity," stressed the moral obligation of institutions to service society and the interconnectedness of economies.

She stated that profit and purpose are not mutually exclusive. "They are two sides of the same coin." Our capacity to reconcile economic expansion with environmental and social advancements is essential for a sustainable future.

Her words incited discussions that significantly impacted policy discussions, resulting in her recognition from organizations and leaders.

The Revisiting Roots

Avantika's visit to her hometown in Uttar Pradesh was one of the most significant events in her post-CEO existence. She was invited to inaugurate the bank's branch in the area. She was overwhelmed with pride at the sight of the branch, which was teeming with activity.

She reconnected with old friends and neighbours during her visit, many of whom had followed her journey with admiration.

Mrs. Mishra, her childhood teacher, stated, "You have demonstrated what is feasible." "Every child in this town is inspired by your narrative."

Avantika also visited her father's old shop, now run by her cousin. Standing there, surrounded by shelves of books and stationery, she felt a profound connection to her beginnings.

The Avantika Agarwal Centre

The Avantika Agarwal Centre for Innovation and Leadership had emerged as a symbol of progress and creativity in Mumbai. From conducting research on sustainable finance to incubating fintech ventures, the centre's programs were diverse.

Avantika randomly visited the centre one day. She observed young professionals in the laboratories brainstorming, their energy reminiscent of her early days. She conversed with a group that was engaged in a project to incorporate blockchain with renewable energy financing during a quiet moment.

"What inspires you to undertake such challenges?" she inquired.

A team member replied, "Because we believe we can make a difference. This centre gives us the tools and support to turn our ideas into impact."

Avantika's heart swelled with pride as she beamed. The centre was a living testament to the values she had championed.

A Quiet Evening

Avantika met with Priya and other members of her erstwhile leadership team one evening. They exchanged anecdotes, reflecting on the obstacles they had encountered and the successes they had attained.

"Do you miss it?" Priya inquired.

Some days," Avantika acknowledged. "However, I am at ease with the knowledge that the bank is in capable hands." Our collaborative efforts have established a foundation that will endure.

Their discussion then shifted to the future of banking and the emergent trends that are influencing the industry. Avantika's passion for innovation remained unwavering, and her insights remained keen even in retirement.

The Chapter Ends

Avantika contemplated her voyage as she prepared for bed that evening. Her life had been a tapestry of challenges, development, and impact, from the small town in Uttar Pradesh to the global stage. She had established a legacy that transcended the confines of a bank, influencing lives and fostering transformation.

In her journal, she wrote:

"True leadership is not about the position you hold but the lives you touch. It is about planting seeds for a future you may never see, trusting that they will grow. I leave this chapter of my life with gratitude, knowing that the journey continues—not just for me but for all who believe in the power of progress."

The epilogue concludes with Avantika turning off her lamp, leaving the room illuminated by the light of a city. The Mumbai skyline, a symbol of resilience and boundless potential, sparkled from the outside.